Ruthless Pursuit

A Vince Dalby Western Adventure - Book 1

William Tresler

Prologue

John "Bullet" Tayes despised the stranger standing on the dry trail. Sweat leaked down the side of his dirty face like sour tar sticking to a dead man's casket. "You best ride on, stranger," John spat.

Vince Dalby remained stiller than a scream caught in the throat of a man preparing to be hanged. His gun hand rested on a Colt Peacemaker. The gun silently hissed like a poisonous snake hiding behind a dry bush. The smell of death was in the air.

John kept his eyes on Vince. Vince was tall and sturdy. The kind of man who could ride bareback on a trail horse while shooting down a herd of buffalo. The man's eyes were hidden under a black hat stained with trail dust. John felt like he was looking at a tombstone rather than a man. "Stranger, you best—"

"Ride on. I heard you." Vince spoke in a gruff, stone-like tone that set John back.

John had been riding wild in the Arizona territory, working as a hired gun for gangs that rustled cattle up from Mexico. John had killed Pete Smithson, a deputy, a month prior. With a reward out for him and a rope waiting for his neck, John was headed for Colorado to stay with his brother.

Two weeks later, he had gotten drunk and gunned down Stanley Green. "You a bounty hunter, stranger? You after me cause I killed Stanley Green? It was a fair fight. I ain't killed no man without cause!" John said.

Vince kept his shadowy eyes locked on John. John reminded him of a barn rat carrying a mouth full of rotted teeth. The only thing John had going for him was his guns. John was quick on the draw. "Does the name Michael O'Neil mean anything?"

John felt his gun hand tense up. "That fella drew on me first! It was a fair fight! Sheriff even said so!"

"Been looking for you, John. Now we play for blood, just like you played for blood with my cousin." Vince slowly spread his feet apart just enough to show John that death was riding down the trail. "Yeah, it was a fair fight. Michael got himself whiskeyed up and ran his mouth some. You could have walked away."

"No man calls me yella and lives!" John felt the taste of grave dirt enter his dry, dirty mouth. He was scared. Word was out that a fella named Vince Dalby was haunting the territory. Vince carried a reputation for being a fearless gunfighter. The man had fought for the Confederate Army during the War Between the States. His reputation was stained with blood. "You best ride on, stranger!"

"You have five seconds to pull your gun," Vince warned.

John quickly spit out a mouth full of tobacco. He took a step back. Vince was going to draw on him. That was clear. The trail was silent. John's horse had moved away toward a dry creek bed. The nearest ranch was three miles away. John was on his own. He went for his gun!

Vince thundered his Colt Peacemaker out of a split holster faster than a rattler could strike a trail hand. The palm of his left hand licked the hammer on his gun three times. Three bullets sliced into the hot air.

One bullet tore through John's forehead. The second and

third bullet ate through his heart. John hit the ground deader than a coffin nail. Blood and pieces of the man's head landed beside his body.

"It's done, Michael. I did what Melinda would have me to do for you." Vince put his gun away with a slow hand. He approached John's body like a mortician preparing to examine an open grave. Half of John's head was torn open. Parts of his skull and pieces of his brain rested on the ground. A grotesque scream was chiseled on the man's face. "Best haul the body into town and—"

A sound.

Vince went for his gun.

A small boy took off from behind a tree like a scalded cat. Vince watched the boy run down the trail as he yelled, "Pa! Pa!" in a scared voice. The boy was barefoot and poorly dressed. Skinny as all get out, too.

Vince put his gun away. He had to tend to the body of John Tayes. Money was tight. The reward for John wasn't much, but the money would help. Finding John's horse didn't take too long. Vince wrapped the dead man's body in a blanket and then tied him over his horse. With that chore done, he set out for Durango.

The sun was starting to grow tired. The heat still buzzed loudly in Vince's ears, but he could feel night approaching in his bones. He needed to reach Durango before the sun set.

After riding a few miles, the trail opened up. Vince spotted a ranch off to his right. The ranch looked poor—dry and hungry.

Vince had heard rumors that a man by the name of Art Lattimere was giving local ranchers trouble. A lot of folks were throwing their weight in gold at Durango. Animas City was starting to suffer. Business owners were relocating to Durango because it was booming. Animas City was drying up, and Art Lattimere had stock in Animas City.

Sheriff Norton Burke had his hands full in Durango. Over

twenty saloons operated in the town. The saloons served trouble each evening. Trail hands hungry for a cheap bottle of whiskey, gamblers looking for a quick dollar, hired guns searching for blood, outlaws hungry to make a name for themselves—the saloons became home to every kind of filthy varmint there was. Sheriff Burke didn't have the time or resources to fiddle with the likes of Art Lattimere.

To make matters worse, there was no lawman in Animas City. Art Lattimere was the law. That was bad. Local ranchers were being hit hard by hired guns. No deaths. Mostly burned barns and bunk houses: warnings.

Vince eyed the poor ranch he had come on as he thought about a conversation he had heard in Animas City a couple of days back while sitting and eating a bowl of soup at the local eatery. The two men sitting in the dining room with him were hired guns. Vince heard one man brag about how he had whipped a rancher with a gun nearly to death. It took every ounce of control Vince had not to call the two hired guns out. Vince was after John. Whatever was happening in Animas City wasn't his fight.

Or was it?

The sound of a woman screaming brought Vince's mind back to the dry trail he was riding on. "Smoke!" he heard the woman scream.

Smoke? Vince didn't see any smoke. Not at first. Then his eyes locked on a shabby barn sitting fifty yards away from the measly ranch house.

"Get the livestock out of the barn!" a man roared.

Vince spotted a man taking off on a wild horse. The man on the horse rode off into a back field and vanished as more smoke began to pour off a barn that was on its last leg.

The sound of scared work horses exploded into the air. Three milk cows began crying. Vince watched a man and woman run into the barn. The skinny boy who had seen him shoot John Tayes followed. A second boy—much younger—trailed behind, carrying a bad limp.

"Get on!" Vince kicked the sides of his horse. He let John's horse be. The horse let out a war cry, stormed off the trail, and began running for the barn. Vince realized the man he had seen running into the barn had a bad limp like his youngest son.

Vince came up on a low cattle fence. He was a man who had ridden into fierce battles countless times, jumping blockades and fences with his gun blaring. He kicked the sides of his horse even harder. The horse picked up speed. The horse was wild as an untamed river and fearless. "Go!" The horse jumped the cattle fence and soared into the hot air like a brazen eagle.

"Pa! Look!" the boy who had seen Vince gun John Tayes down yelled as he kicked a pig out of a barn that was quickly starting to burn.

The man spotted a stranger riding up. Before he could say a word, Vince was off his horse and ready for action. "Got to get the work horses out of the barn, mister!"

Vince nodded. "Keep your family out here!" Vince yanked a black bandana off his neck and ran into the barn. The flames inside the barn were spreading like snake venom coursing through the blood of a wounded man. Vince heard horses screaming. He went to work freeing the horses and then focused his attention on the milk cows.

When Vince ran the last of the milk cows out, the younger boy cried, "Jasper is still in the barn. He's tied up near the back where I keep him. He has a hurt leg!"

"The barn is burning too bad!" the woman screamed. "The beams are sure to give at any minute!"

Vince knew she was right. The fire eating the barn was fierce. No matter. He wasn't the type of man to leave an animal to burn alive. He threw his right arm over in front of his face and raced *back into the flames. Th smoke was so thick, Vince couldn't breathe. The flames were so hot, he felt like his face would burn down to the bone. Where was the horse? In the back... yeah... in the back of the barn.*

A burning beam crashed down. Vince dived over the burning beam and managed to roll back onto his legs. A second beam crashed down. Vince ran to the back of the barn.

"Get back!" the man yelled at his wife and two sons. He rushed his family back as the barn began to give in. "That man ain't gonna come out of there alive!"

With terrified eyes, the family watched the barn collapse and burn. A few minutes later, Vince came walking through the smoke, coughing but alive. His right hand was connected to a rope that was wrapped around a frightened pinto horse.

"Jasper!" The boy quickly limped toward Vince.

Vince handed him the rope he was holding. "Here's your horse, son." He coughed as fresh air stung his lungs.

The boy's parents ran to Vince. "He has some burns," the woman said.

"I'll leave, ma'am," Vince grunted.

"Mister, you were crazy to run into that fire. You could have gotten yourself burned alive," the man scolded Vince as he wiped sweat off his forehead. "You the man who gunned down John Tayes?" Miles pointed at his older son. "Logan said he saw you gun John Tayes down."

"Your boy saw right."

"You a bounty hunter?" he demanded.

"When I need to be," Vince answered.

"What does that mean? Either you're a bounty hunter or you ain't, mister."

Vince locked his eyes on the burning barn. "Saw a man riding off just before the barn went up."

"Yeah... my barn ain't gonna be the last, either." The man put

his arm over his wife's shoulder. He eyed Vince. "John Tayes was fast on the draw. My boy said you put three bullets in him. Said the first bullet nearly tore John's head slap off. If what my boy said is true, we could use a man like you around here. Trouble ain't brewing, mister. Trouble is here."

Vince could sense this was a good man. A decent sort. But not the type of man who could fight wild guns on his own. "I got to get to Durango and see Sheriff Burke."

"Mister, you best be careful. Word was John Tayes was working for Art Lattimere. You best watch your back." The man turned to face his burning barn. "We best let the barn burn out, Lauretta."

"And then what?" Lauretta begged. "We wait until Lattimere burns our home down? This was a warning, Miles, for us to leave."

"We ain't leaving our home." Miles pulled his wife even closer. "I ain't no coward. Couldn't live with myself if I let the likes of Lattimere run me off."

"Can you live with yourself if you end up six feet under the ground?" Lauretta began to cry.

Vince watched Logan step close to his brother. Logan looked at Vince through a pair of desperate eyes that begged him to stay. "Yeah... I reckon this body can wait until tomorrow. Mind if I bunk down here tonight?" he asked Miles.

"Stay at your own risk, mister."

Vince nodded. He looked at Logan. Logan's eyes told Vince that the only way his pa was ever going to have peace on his land was if Art Lattimere was six feet under the ground. A new scent of blood entered the hot air as night began to fall.

In the distance, a hidden rider watched Vince standing beside his horse. He spit and then rode off to tell his boss that Vince wasn't going to ride off any time soon.

Chapter One

The smell of hot smoke kept a dry air drunk with violence as Vince Dalby secured the horse of Tayes to a horse line he had run between two trees. The south end of Miles Harter's ranch was close to the main trail Vince had ridden in on.

Night had fallen. The trail was dark. It wasn't likely anyone would mess with the dead man Vince had shot dead. "Settle down," Vince said to the horse as his eyes listened to the darkness rather than his ears.

The darkness was a familiar friend to Vince. How many nights had he moved through dark woods, advancing toward enemy territory, during the War Between the States? How many Union soldiers had he slipped up on unseen and unheard and killed without mercy?

How much blood had stained his hands? Inside of Vince's mind, he heard the sound of death enter a man as he slid a sharp blade across a dirty neck. Vince could still smell the blood. Hear the fear. See the death he had created.

After putting the body between a couple of dry bushes and covering it with a blanket, Vince walked back to the Harter's ranch, walking over hard ground that held no mercy—ground that was always thirsty for water and grass.

Hard, angry dirt hissed at Vince as he walked toward a ranch house that resembled a dead cry rather than a signal of hope.

Miles was standing outside on the front porch having a smoke of tobacco. "Get that scalawag settled down for the night?" he asked. His right hand was holding a corncob pipe filled with tobacco... Miles could only afford the cheap stuff.

"Reckon that dead snake ain't goin' nowhere tonight." Vince leaned against a wooden porch railing as he answered Miles. Overhead, a sea of stars whispered sweet secrets. Vince liked to see the stars. Somewhere above them, he knew God was watching.

Miles wasn't a threatening man. He wasn't tall and deadly like Vince. He was the type of man who had a hardworking face and determined eyes—but not the eyes of a man who could bring the blade of a knife across another man's throat.

Miles wasn't a coward by any means. He would fight and die for his family at any given second, sure enough. But he just wasn't the type of man who hungered for blood. "Your supper is on the table," Miles told Vince. "Wife made beans. Ain't much, but fills the well when the well is dry."

Vince smelled Miles's pipe. The smell brought memories of his own pa smoking a pipe. "You got trouble, Miles."

"I ain't cuttin' and runnin'."

"Didn't think you would." Vince kept his eyes on the open land, searching the darkness, listening. His right hand was resting on a split holster, inside the holster, a hungry Colt Peacemaker. "What are you thinking?"

"Reckon I'm thinking what the other ranchers are thinking," Miles answered without putting up much of a worry. The work clothes covering his back still smelled of smoke and sweat. Miles didn't care.

He only had the one pair of work clothes and his best going to church suit his wife Lauretta kept, hanging in a back room. "Art Lattimere is right determined to run us off our land because we're not paying up. He's got the money to hire guns to do it, too. My barn was a warning."

"Pay up?"

Miles tapped his pipe against a porch railing and then took a seat on a wooden chair he sat down in to whittle wood when his mind was troubled. The chair creaked and moaned under the sea of stars. "You sure you want to know why my barn was burned?"

Vince nodded without speaking a word.

"Okay, then." Miles folded his arms together. "Art Lattimere is the big bug around these parts. He owns the biggest spread. Most of the ranchers, including me... well, we're just small-timers. Oh, I reckon I run a good herd every now and then, but just enough to pay my land tax and put food on the table. Lately, I haven't even been able to run a good herd."

"Lattimere?"

"Cut down my cattle fence. Most of my herd got loose. Lattimere branded the loose heads before I could claim them" Anger tinted his voice. "Life was good around these parts before Lattimere showed up. A man who called himself Big Dave owned Lattimere's spread. Sold his spread to Lattimere after his son was killed."

Vince waited.

"Most folks believe Lattimere was behind the killing. Ain't got no way to prove it."

"Your wife said you were a deputy in Durango."

Miles patted a sore leg. "You seen me limping? Got in a tussle with one of Lattimere's hired guns in the Burning Bullet Saloon. Bunch of Lattimere's guns were in the saloon, all whiskeyed up and hungry for a fight." He touched his sore leg and then shrugged his shoulders. What could he do? His leg would heal in time. "Sheriff Burke and me went in to settle matters down after shooting was heard. A trail snake named Harry Jones drew his gun on me. I shot him dead, but he got a bullet into my leg first."

"Bad?"

"Doc Cunningham took the bullet out. Said the bullet nipped a bone. I'll be limping for a while. Don't reckon the leg will ever be the same. Could be worse. I could be sleeping six feet under in a wooden box tonight."

Vince respected Miles's attitude. The man aimed straight and fired hard. No sense in complaining. Just ride while you can and make sure you ride right and die good. "Lattimere didn't take kindly to killing one of his guns, I suspect."

"Nope." Miles shook his head. "I ain't the killing type. Reckon if Harry Jones had been sober, I would have shook hands with death instead of him. I ain't slow at the draw, but I ain't the fastest, either. I know my limits. Lattimere doesn't hire slow guns."

"You're taking time away from your badge."

"Have to. When another man smells weakness on a man, he goes for the kill. Durango is growing. That's good. But that also means a lot of hard trail riders are riding in. Sheriff Burke decided its best if I tend to my ranch." Miles went silent for a minute. "Sheriff Burke still sends me out my pay. Ain't right for him to do so since I ain't wearing my badge. Pay ain't much, but it helps when my herds are dry as brown grass."

"Hard work being a deputy and a rancher."

"I ranch during the day and deputy at night. Used to sleep in the jail. Always hated leaving my family out here alone. Bothered me to no end. Sometimes I thank the Good Lord that I was shot. Then again... I think about my friend Sheriff Burke and the troubles he's facing. The horizon is filled with blood. I fear it's just a matter of time before Lattimere tries to gun down Sheriff Burke."

"If I ain't mistaken, the Denver and Rio Grande Railroad have dug in its spurs in this part of the land."

"Sure enough." Miles thought for a minute. "The tracks from Durango to Silverton got finished last month. Big to-do about it, too. Goal for the railroad is to reach the mines way up there in the San Juan Mountains. Lots of ore up that way. Good way to make a man rich. Railroad wants to haul ore down to smelters that are being built in Durango."

"What about Animas?"

"Last year, the Denver and Rio Grande Railway decided to build Durango. Durango is putting a hurting on Animas. Animas was the big-shot town before the railroad decided to build Durango. Won't be long, I reckon, before Animas becomes nothing but a dusty hole on the trail. Like I said, when ore starts being hauled from Silverton to Durango... well, Animas won't last. Folks go where the work is. I'll hold out as long as I can. Folks need beef."

Vince grew silent.

"The railroad ran forty-five miles of track up the Animas River to Silverton. I reckon Animas might hang on a bit, but in my opinion, it won't. I don't know what the railroad has planned for Animas. All I know is that folks are leaving Animas and moving to Durango. Folks go where the work and money is."

Vince chewed on a thought. "There's more than ore up in the San Juan Mountains."

"Gold and silver," Miles stated in a matter-of-fact tone. "Seen some of the gold and silver with my own eyes. Rumors are the railroad just wants to let folks do a little sightseeing and all. Folks know the truth. The railroad wants to bleed the mines in this part of the land dry. Ain't nothing anyone can do about it. The railroad has the rights. Besides, folks need work. Families got to eat."

Vince didn't know much about the Denver and Rio Grande Railroad. Little pieces of gunpowder in his mind here and there. Little pieces of gunpowder collected properly could line deadly bullets. Ore, gold, and silver amounted to tons of money. "Lattimere?"

"Thought about that." Miles rubbed his sore leg as the smell of smoke stained his nose. He glanced toward the black piles of smoldering wood that had once been a barn. "Reckon I ain't sure what Lattimere is thinking."

"Mind telling me what your thoughts are?"

"Vince, you're asking for trouble," Miles warned. "This part of the land ain't your home. You're just passing through. Ain't no sense in making hard fists at a snake like Lattimere."

"Let me worry about that."

Miles stared at Vince. Vince had his eyes on the night. The man was hard and fierce, that much was certain. But there was more to the man. Miles sensed that Vince had some smarts to him. "Well, it's like this. Lattimere is having his hired guns going around to collect what he calls protection money. If you pay up, then Lattimere promises to play nice. If you don't pay up, then..." Miles tossed a thumb toward his burned barn. "Lattimere runs Animas with a hard hand."

"No law in Animas."

"Sheriff Burke was the law. He took to Durango when he got offered higher pay. No one blamed him. Animas didn't have much trouble before Lattimere arrived. Wearing a badge didn't pay for a bag of beans. Sheriff Burke has a wife and a boy."

"The railroad?"

Miles shrugged his shoulders. "The railroad has Lattimere outgunned. Lattimere is trail dust compared to the big bugs who own the railroad. He knows that, too. But you know, Vince... in my thinking, and I don't think of myself as a learned man who can read all of them fancy books, it seems to me that a scalawag like Lattimere would want to get in on the goods while he can."

Vince didn't argue the point. He decided to learn more about the Denver and Rio Grande Railroad. Vince knew the railroads had brought some good—but the railroads also brought blood, violence, and destruction to the land. "Miles, mind if I stay on a bit?"

"Can't pay you."

"A plate of beans will be enough."

Miles locked his eyes on Vince's gun hand. "I ain't got much cattle to run. Just a few heads. I can do that myself with my two boys."

"I'll do what I can."

"Seems to me, in my thinking, you're worried that if you ride off and come back in a few months, me and my family might be dead," Miles pointed out. "Appreciate the concern, but I can take care of my own."

"I found John Tayes on his way to your ranch. Could you have gunned him down in a fair fight?" Vince asked.

Miles rubbed the back of a sore neck. "Nope," he offered an honest answer. "Didn't know John Tayes was on his way to my ranch, either."

"Can't be sure, but he was heading this way. Makes sense that maybe Lattimere was sending him to roughen you up. Maybe Lattimere burned your barn down after I killed Tayes?"

"Could be." Miles closed his eyes. He had seen John Tayes around. Tayes was a killer. Miles knew the man was faster at the draw than he was. What if Tayes had arrived on his ranch and forced Miles to go for his gun? Tayes would have gunned him down. Miles's oldest boy, Logan, would have run for his rifle. Tayes would have put a bullet in the boy's back and then dragged his wife off to Lattimere. Lattimere, Miles knew, had an eye for his wife. Miles's youngest boy would have tried to stop Tayes. Tayes would have shot the boy dead.

Vince heard Miles groan. He knew what the man was thinking. "Mind if I stay on?"

"This ain't your fight."

"It is now."

"Why?" Miles demanded. "You're just a stranger riding through."

"Not anymore." Vince turned to face Miles. "My pa raised his family up in the Georgia mountains. Nothing but poor farmers struggling to put food on the table. Folks took care of each other. When the crops were weak, folks shared what they had. That's just the way it was."

"Yeah, that's the way it should be." Miles nodded.

"When the War Between the States started, I was too young to fight. I waited two hard years. Thought I was going to miss the fighting." Vince's voice turned hard. "Impressed an officer with my riding and shooting skills. When I got asked about my age, I lied straight out. Before I knew it, I was fighting hard and killing hard. At night, me and some other fellas would sneak into the enemy camp and hunt down officers. Sabotage the artillery. Steal horses. I was young, but I knew how to kill and I knew how to stay alive."

Miles listened.

"I killed without mercy. I was strong, silent... determined." Blood filled Vince's mind. "It got to where I had to kill. I couldn't rest unless I killed a man. Word got around about how savage I had gotten. An officer tried to settle me down, but I just got worse."

"Killing can do that to a man."

Vince nodded. "One night, I sneaked into the enemy's camp alone. I heard two brothers talking. They were sitting around a

16

campfire on watch. The night was cold. A hard snow was falling. I listened to them talk about their families... how they hated the war... how they wanted to go home. They weren't no older than I was."

"You killed them?"

"Yeah... no mercy." Vince slowly opened his eyes. "I set some tents on fire and cut some horse lines."

"Yeah..." Miles could sense that Vince was telling him why he wasn't going to ride off.

"After we lost Gettysburg, I knew the war was over. Couldn't stand the thought of seeing the enemy take over my home. I rode with a few hard men for a while, striking at the enemy when we could. We got chased into Arkansas. Union Army caught up to us one night. A hard fight followed. Out of twenty-five men, only me and another fella made it out alive."

"And you went west?"

"With blood in my eyes," Vince confessed. He turned back to the stars. "Met a woman in Texas. Wasn't long before that woman became my wife." Vince lowered his head. "My wife took out all the blood in me. Can't explain how, but she did."

"Your wife is dead?"

"Killed during a bank robbery." Vince gritted his teeth. "That's when I sold the land we had in Texas and became a hunter again. Hunted down the man who killed my wife and gunned him down real hard."

"Didn't help, did it?" Miles asked.

"No," Vince confessed. "My wife begged me before she died to start doing what was right. She told me that helping folks was better than killing men I hated. Reckon she was right because those two fellas I killed... the brothers... they still torment me to this day. Had no right to kill them. Had no right to kill lots of the men I did during the war."

Miles knew Vince was finished. The man had said enough.

"If you want to stay on, I reckon I would appreciate the notion. Don't reckon Lattimere is going to look the other way now that he has his sights on my ranch. But I best tell you that, when you go into Durango to turn over John Tayes, you best talk to Sheriff Burke. Taking the law into your own hands ain't the way out here. When a man steps outside of the law, he becomes no better than the trail snakes he's fighting."

"You say that after your family was put in harm's way."

"I say that because if I become what the men I hate are, then I'm showing my boys that the only things that matter in this life are bullets. I want my boys to learn that a man doesn't have to kill in order to live. I know death is all around these parts... but when a man strives to work hard and live in peace, well, I reckon that's better than being fast on the draw."

Miles's answer settled into Vince's gut like a hard stone. "I'll talk to Sheriff Burke when I ride into Durango tomorrow. You coming?"

"Reckon I will. My sister-in-law will be riding out here tomorrow. She always visits with her lady friends once a week. Ain't no reason for me to be here, seeing how all I hear is talk about leaving this part of the land." Miles struggled to stand up. "Appreciate you telling me what you did. I've seen fellas tormented by the war. Some went to their graves deader than the bullets that killed them. Seems to me you're looking for what my wife calls... What was the word she used? Oh yeah... absolution."

"What is that?" Vince asked.

"Well, the way my wife explained it, absolution is what happens when a fella wants to be free from what's tormenting him." He tapped the thigh of his bad leg. "Well, I reckon I'm going to go on back inside. Your supper is on the table. The bunk house ain't much, but there's a couple of straw beds and a blanket."

Vince listened as Miles limped into the ranch house. He wasn't sure why he had told Miles about his days during the war. It just seemed to Vince that Miles needed to know what kind of man he had been and what kind of man he was. "I reckon in time... when death comes for me... I'll know if I have that absolution or not. In the meantime, I got work to do."

The smell of smoke continued to stain the hot night air. Vince stayed on the front porch for a while and then made his weary way into the bunkhouse without eating his supper.

Chapter Two

A hard rain arrived during the night. The rain followed into early morning hours but waned off as Vince tied the body of John Tayes to his horse. The smell of wet dirt and danger drifted through the morning air like a skilled law man watching the hand of a bloody outlaw.

Vince sensed trouble riding down the trail. He glanced over at Miles. Miles was sitting on a sleepy quarter horse that didn't look anxious to walk ten steps let alone travel a hard trail to Durango. Miles looked as sleepy and worn down as his horse.

"That's it." Vince spoke as he tightened a strap for a saddle rope. "We better ride."

Miles watched Vince check the saddle on his own horse before mounting. Vince's horse was a powerful mountain in Miles's eyes. The horse's eyes were familiar with the sounds of battle and men dying. "We best get a wiggle on, that's for sure. Durango isn't an easy ride."

Vince checked Tayes's horse and made sure the rope he was holding was strong. He didn't have to gig his horse. Vince's horse started forward on his own. The horse knew Vince better than Vince knew himself. It seemed to Miles. Vince studied the trail as he rode forward. There were lots of places on the trail to ambush a rider.

"Wife wanted me to ask you if you've ever been in a gospel mill?" Miles asked Vince.

"My pa read the Good Book to us when I was a boy," Vince answered, keeping his voice low. His two Cold Peacemakers were watchful. His saddle rifle—a Yellowboy, a name Vince didn't care for—was prepared for action. Vince's tone told Miles not to press the subject.

"I can tell my wife I asked."

"Yeah…" Vince didn't say any more. He moved on down the trail, slow but steady.

Miles covered the rear. The land was hard. Rough. Unforgiving. The trail was muddy and difficult.

About half an hour into the ride, three horses appeared down the trail. Vince slowed his pace. He eyed the riders on the horse. Thirsty trees, boulders, and hungry trail brush hugged the trail. A few high hills had formed off the sides. Perfect spot for an ambush.

"Get your rifle," Vince ordered Miles.

Miles went for a newer rifle than the one Vince owned. His rifle had been made no more than nine years back. Miles was grateful for his Winchester rifle. He was about the same with a rifle as with a gun, but a rifle just felt better in his hands. "Those are Lattimere's boys."

"Yeah…" Vince slowed to a stop as the three riders started to approach. He drew out his rifle with skilled hands. As soon as the three riders drew close enough, he fired a warning shot into the air. "Far enough. State your business."

Gary Cappes, Ed Newman, and Dan Mufford—three dirty, whiskey-eyed trail snakes glared at Vince through eyes that were familiar with bullying and cold-blooded murder. Not a single man went for his gun or rifle, though. They were on the trail to deliver a message.

"Boss has a message for you," Ed Newman stated in a taunting voice. He spit black juice out of his rotted mouth and then ran a dirty arm covered with a black coat across a filthy black beard.

Vince sat steady and firm as he watched each man. "I said state your business and then ride on."

Ed pointed at Miles. "You should have paid up, boy."

Vince fired a second shot into the air. "My last warning."

Ed scowled. "You best ride on," he spat at Vince. "The boss don't take kindly to the likes of you, and he ain't about to higgle with you either. You can ride on or end up dead."

Gary Cappes pulled out a quirley. He lit it with a dirty hand. "I should kill you for gunning down ol' Tayes. I liked him. He was the only one who could cheat at cards and get away with it."

"Go for your gun," Vince dared Gary.

Gary took a draw from his quirley. "Ain't here to kill... not today. Boss sent us to tell you to scat. You got until sundown."

Gary was just as filthy as his riding partners, but Vince sensed he was the smartest one of the three. It was time to rile the man's temper. "Seen you in Texas. You gunned down William Frayes."

"Fair fight," Gary told Vince.

"Frayes was whiskeyed up. You were stone sober," Vince told Gary. "You only kill a man who can't walk straight?"

A cruel frown formed on Gary's face. "You sayin' something you shouldn't?"

"I'm calling you yellow." Vince spoke clearly and without hesitation.

Miles tensed up. Was Vince trying to make Lattimere's men

draw on him? It sure seemed that way. "We're just riding into Durango, boys. No need for trouble."

"Trouble is here, boy." Gary threw down his quirley. He locked eyes with Vince. "I came to give you a message. I did my job. Now it's just between us. Get off your horse!"

"That dog won't hunt with the boss," Ed told Gary. "We ain't here to draw our shootin' irons. Not yet. Boss sent us with a message to give. He don't want any more bloodshed right now."

"You gonna keep wobblin' your jaw or let him stay yellow?" Vince asked Ed.

Gary jumped off his horse. No one called him yellow. No one! "I play for blood."

Vince saddled his rifle and then dismounted. He handed the horse rope he was holding to Miles without saying a word and then stepped away from the horses. Ed and Dan glanced at each other.

"His fight," Dan told Ed, and then forced his horse to take a few steps back. Ed did the same. When two men were determined to kill, there wasn't anything to do but wait until death crawled up out of the ground.

Miles knew he was caught in a bad box. All he could do was watch Vince's back. "You boys stand down," he told Ed and Dan. "This fight ain't yours or mine."

Ed and Dan didn't object.

Gary flipped the ends of the black coat he was wearing away from his gun belt. "You're one of them cowardly rebels," he spat at Vince. "I fought in the war. We whipped you rebels so bad, you went cryin' home like yellow-belly cowards."

Vince eyed Gary as dark shadows began covering his eyes. Gary was a cold-blooded murderer. A man who hungered for blood—just like Vince had once hungered for blood. In reality, Vince wasn't much different from Gary. The only difference was Vince was searching for what Miles's wife called absolution.

Gary snarled. His teeth were black, his eyes yellow from drinking too much rotgut. Vince's eyes were sober and clear. Sharp. Alert. Prepared. Gary was still suffering from a night of too much heavy drinking. He didn't care. He hated rebels. "Die, you filthy rebel—" he yelled as he went for his guns without warning.

Vince had his gun drawn before Gary's firing hand could get within three inches of his gun. All Ed and Dan saw was two bullets open up the back of Gary's head and then Gary drop dead on the trail, the same way John Tayes had dropped dead.

"You best ride on!" Ed yelled and then spurred his horse. "Get on now!" Ed's horse let out a cry and then turned and fired down the trail.

Dan pointed at Vince. "You're a dead man!" Dan yelled, and then turned his attention to Miles. "You best prepare, boy!" he warned, and then spurred his horse.

Vince watched Dan ride off. He put his gun away.

Miles looked angry. "Now why did you go and crawl that fella's hump for? You know he was fit to be tied. It was best just to leave him be," Miles told Vince. "Now Lattimere is going to really try to tan my hide."

"Lattimere ain't gonna go away, Miles. Best to take out his best gun while you can." Vince kicked dirt onto Gary's dead face. "Seen this varmint fight before. Know his kind. He's bloodthirsty. Best to kill him now."

"Vince, Lattimere has more guns."

Vince walked to the horse Miles was sitting on. He looked up at the man. "You fight when you can, Miles. You let the enemy know you're not afraid. If you want to turn yellow, then ride off."

"I ain't yellow!" Miles snapped at Vince. "I just don't see no need to make Lattimere mad."

"Lattimere didn't burn down your barn because he wants to be your friend."

Miles opened his mouth and then just shook his head in frustration. He looked down at Gary's body. Miles had never seen a man get shot through the head before. He could smell blood and bits and pieces of brain. "You best get that body roped up."

Vince left Miles alone. Miles wasn't a soldier. He didn't understand that you killed a wild snake when you could. Vince wanted to wound Lattimere. He knew Lattimere had sent his three best men out onto the trail. You didn't send slow guns to deliver a message to a deadly gunslinger. With Gary Cappes dead, Vince had sent a clear message to Lattimere while showing his best guns just how capable he was of killing.

After tying Gary's body to his horse, Vince rode on to Durango without any more trouble shooting at him. Durango looked like any other dusty town to Vince. Yeah, the town was being built up, but the town was still a young calf.

There seemed to be more saloons than sense. The streets were muddy. The buildings—although still redolent with the fading scent of fresh-cut lumber—resembled lifeless tombstones.

In Vince's eyes, Durango wasn't any different from Tombstone, Arizona. Tombstone was a young calf, too, full of violence and blood. Vince had encountered some wild scorpions in Tombstone.

He had been in the town when Wyatt Earp and his brothers, along with a man who was known as Doc Holiday—heavy drinker and gambler—went gun to gun with some wild scorpions. Three men ended up dead. Vince had seen one of the dead men the day prior. Death came fast.

Durango made Vince think of every other dusty, thirsty

town he had ridden into. What was a town, anyway, Vince wondered. A home? Vince didn't know where home was anymore.

"Jail is this way. Tracks over the east of town. Ain't no trains in town today. Tracks are empty." Miles told Vince as he watched men on horseback and women walking on wooden walkways attached to the front of buildings toss worried or hard eyes at the two horses Vince was pulling behind him. The dead man strapped across each horse lay in silence.

Vince followed Miles to the end of a muddy street. Miles stopped in front of a building that held no windows. A wooden sign was nailed to the front of the building. The word "Jail" had been burned into the sign. Vince dismounted. His back ached from the hard ride. He wanted a drink but had vowed to his dead wife to remain dry to his dying day.

Sheriff Norton Burke stepped out of the jail carrying a rifle. His eyes fell onto the two bodies Vince had hauled into town. "Miles," Sheriff Burke nodded at Miles. "What's this?"

Miles remained on his horse. More and more eyes were looking toward the jail. A man and woman traveling on a worn-down horse buggy that probably cost less than the sense they had stopped, examined the scene, and then moved on. "Best ask this man. His name is Vince Dalby."

"Mr. Dalby, what's this all about?"

Vince looked at Sheriff Burke. The man was tall and thin. His face was smart and watchful. He was the type of man who believed in using deadly force only when necessary. When calmer heads could prevail, then so be it. "That's the body of John Tayes. There's a bounty out on him. The other body belongs to a man who challenged me to a gun fight on the trail. Miles can speak for me."

Sheriff Burke had a look at the two bodies. "This man is

Gary Cappes..." Sheriff Burke covered the body back up. "You best come into the jail with me," he told Vince.

"I'm going to get some supplies. Just need some sugar and flour," Miles told Sheriff Burke.

Sheriff Burke felt bad for Miles. Miles only had enough money to buy enough sugar and flour to carry home in the saddle bags attached to his horse. He flipped Miles a dollar coin. "See you when you get back."

"Now listen—" Miles began to object.

"See you in a bit." Sheriff Burke walked Vince into the jail. He lodged his rifle onto a rack and then rested behind a wooden desk. "See that."

Vince looked at a wall holding wanted posters. "Doesn't take long, does it?"

"Not in this territory," Sheriff Burke answered. "Durango is just shallow water right now. It won't be long before the railroad turns this town into something big. Town already has a bank. That's a nice target."

"I'm not bringing trouble."

"I don't like bounty hunters."

Vince knew what Sheriff Burke was aiming at. "I came for John Tayes. Found out a man named Lattimere is giving Miles Harter and his family a hard time."

Sheriff Burke leaned back on a squeaky wooden chair and studied Vince. Vince held the face of a man who had killed his fair share of men. "See this jail?"

Vince looked around the dry room. An old wood stove stood in the middle of the room. A closed door leading back to three holding cells rested at the back of the room. "Not much to it. Never is."

"Maybe not, but this jail is a sign of law and order," Sheriff Burke stated in a stern tone as he removed a brown hat, revealing a thin head of brown hair. "I don't like Lattimere anymore than Miles does, but I ain't got no means to arrest the man."

"Yeah..."

"What did Miles tell you about Lattimere?" Sheriff Burke asked.

Vince grabbed a wooden chair and rested his back. He told Sheriff Burke what he knew. Sheriff Burke listened. "Gary Cappes drew on me first," he finished.

"And you gunned down one of Lattimere's best men," Sheriff Burke stated. "My gut tells me that's what you were aiming for."

Vince didn't answer. He didn't have to.

Sheriff Burke stood up. He walked to the jail door. "Lattimere has a long arm," he warned Vince. "He has men right here in Durango. One of his men controls the land office across the way. Lattimere controls the land office in Animas, too. He's bumping heads real hard with the railroad."

Vince thought for a minute. Was Lattimere holding back land for the railroad? Maybe. But if that was so, why did Sheriff Burke make it seem that Lattimere was kicking spurs into the railroad? What was Lattimere's plan? "The railroad won't put up with the likes of Lattimere for long."

"You would think so." Sheriff Burke went back to his seat. "The line in this area is new. It runs up into the San Juan Mountains."

"Miles told me."

"Then you know the railroad wants to start mining ore, silver, and gold, and running it down this way."

Vince nodded. "Money is always the reason to destroy the land."

"Look, I don't like the railroad any more than Miles, but the fact is this land is expanding. You ain't gonna keep the greedy hands of people off this land. If I had my choice, there wouldn't even be a railroad. Never had a complaint against my horse." Sheriff Burke leaned forward and clasped his hands together. The sheriff's badge connected to the brown button-up shirt he was wearing flashed. "The fact is Durango is going to grow no matter what I do or don't do."

"So you decided it was better to get on board."

"I have a family. I have to earn a living. Being the sheriff in Animas didn't pay me enough to buy a bag of flour." Sheriff Burke eyed Vince. "My pa was a law man. Being a law man is all I know. Durango needs a sheriff."

"You're short a deputy."

Sheriff Burke studied Vince's eyes and then leaned back. "You offering to take over for Miles while his leg heals up?"

"Reckon it wouldn't hurt." Vince folded his arms across his chest. He looked like a shadow wearing all black. Vince knew the sheriff wasn't certain about him. "I saw the fear in the eyes of a scared woman and two scared boys, Sheriff Burke. Miles can't protect his family the way he needs."

"And you want to—"

"I already sent Lattimere a message. I'm not riding off," Vince cut Sheriff Burke off. "Now whether I wear a badge or not... that's up to you."

Sheriff Burke stood up and walked to the wall holding the wanted posters. "You from the south?"

Vince nodded.

"Fought in the war?"

Vince nodded again.

"Lots of men from the war come out this way... from the north and the south. Broken, angry... riding empty trails. Most end up dead." Sheriff Burke turned to face Vince. "Where are you riding to?"

"I don't know." Vince gave an honest answer.

"Whenever your bullets take you, is that it?"

Vince stood up. "For now," he answered, and then pointed at the jail door. "I'll be collecting the bounty now and moving on—"

"You'll get your bounty for the body. But first..." Sheriff Burke drew in a long, careful breath. "But first you best hold up your right hand so I can swear you in."

"You sure?" Vince asked.

"Just as long as you know that once you put on your badge, you're inside the law, not outside."

"Is that where you want me?"

"For a man like you... yeah." Sheriff Burke nodded. "Now hold up your right hand."

Vince held up his right hand. What choice did he have?

While Sheriff Burke deputized Vince, Ed and Dan rode onto a large spread like wild streaks of lightning. Both men had stopped on the trail to get whiskeyed up before dealing with Lattimere. Gary was dead. Lattimere was going to demand blood. Ed and Dan didn't want to face Lattimere sober.

Lattimere heard two horses ride up to the front of his ranch house. He was sitting behind a desk positioned in the corner of a large living room planted with expensive furnishings that brandished power and money. Two horses. Not three. Why not three? Lattimere tossed down a legal document he was holding and reached for a bottle of whiskey. He waited.

Ed and Dan walked through the front door of the ranch house, smelling like the whiskey Lattimere was about to drink. They spotted their boss sitting behind his desk. A large man. Built like a bear. Mean. Vicious. Deadly on the draw.

"Where's Gray?" Lattimere asked before taking a swig of whiskey.

"Dead. Vince Dalby put two bullets through his head," Ed answered without showing much care about Lattimere's response. Whiskey made Ed feel mean—real mean.

Lattimere's temper flared at his drunken employees, but he held back. "On the trail?"

Dan tossed the brown hat he was wearing onto a table that sat beside the front door and then moseyed over to Lattimere's desk. He had faced Lattimere's anger sober once. He figured he would rather die drunk than be beaten with a branding iron again. "We gotta put some bullets into Vince Dalby," he told Lattimere.

"Who else saw the killing?" Lattimere took another swig of whiskey instead of gunning down Ed and Dan on the spot.

"Miles," Ed answered as he joined Dan.

Lattimere's dark eyes began to drip with deadly venom. He despised Miles. "So Miles hired him a gun." Lattimere slammed the whiskey bottle down so hard, whiskey jumped out of the bottle.

Ed and Dan stared at Lattimere. The man was dressed in a fancy gray suit that made him look really smart. The only problem was Lattimere's face. Lattimere shaved every morning. He kept his bear-like face clean in order to come across as a smart rooster. Lattimere was determined to present himself as the type of man who could spin a web just enough to lure in fools before showing his true nature. Any trail rider with a penny's worth of sense could see Lattimere was a cold-blooded killer, though. Lattimere wasn't fooling anyone. It didn't matter how much Lattimere kept his brown hair slicked back or how much he tried to make his hard face appealing. His eyes gave him away. The eyes always gave a man away.

"What's the plan, boss?" Ed asked. "Do we kill them?"

Lattimere locked his eyes on Ed's gun belt. Ed was his number one man now that Gary was dead. "Go into Durango.

Talk to Sheriff Burke. Claim Dalby killed Gary in cold blood. Judge Reed will be in Durango in a few days. Better we try to make sure Dalby ends up at the end of a rope. Too much is at stake to kill him right out."

Ed and Dan nodded their heads. Neither man was in a hurry to end up as worm food. After seeing Gary get gunned down, Ed and Dan both knew Vince was a deadly gun to stand clear of. But while whiskeyed up, they talked bravely. "We'll keep an eye on that trail snake, boss. Let's go, Dan!"

Lattimere watched Ed and Dan leave and then went for the whiskey bottle. "Lauretta will be mine, Miles. It's just a matter of time. When your hired gun ends up at the end of a rope, I'm coming for your wife... only after I kill you myself."

Chapter Three

Night dropped like a heavy blanket over Durango. The saloons in town lit up like usual. Decent folk went home before the sunset. Only the rowdy scalawags stayed in town in order to drink whiskey and play cards.

Vince had seen Ed and Dan ride into town shortly before supper. Both men tied their horses up in front of the Burning Bullet Saloon—a nasty saloon owned by an ex-Union soldier who had barely escaped being hanged for knifing a man to death.

The Burning Bullet was nothing more than a watering hole for soulless creatures destined for violent graves.

Vince had seen Miles off after Ed and Dan rode into Durango. "I got to get back to my family," Miles told Vince as he mounted his horse. Jim Horton and Bob Phillips had ridden into Durango for supplies. Both men were ranchers and friends of Miles. "Jim and Bob will be riding back with me."

Jim was sitting at the front of a wooden wagon loaded with supplies. Bob was sitting next to him. Bob was holding a rifle. The man looked like any other roughneck in town, but his eyes carried an honest glow.

"Best be getting on," Jim spoke in a gruff voice. He didn't want to be seen talking to Vince.

Miles trailed behind the wooden wagon, carrying a deep worry and a pair of watchful eyes. Vince wanted to ride back to Miles's ranch, but decided to stay in town and see if Ed and Dan would try to follow him. When Ed and Dan remained in the saloon, Vince decided to stay in town.

"Time to take a walk," Sheriff Burke told Vince as he grabbed his rifle. "Don't take long for the saloons to get rowdy."

Vince followed Sheriff Burke out into a dark night filled with air that felt like it had been baked in a hot oven. To the east, he could see lightning painting the landscape with ghostly hands. A tough storm was moving toward Durango.

Vince studied the front street. All the buildings except for the saloons were dark. A few men—mostly ranch vermin who were anxious to drink away their pay—stood out on wooden walkways in small groups, talking and taking swigs from cheap whiskey bottles. It was too hot to sit inside for most of the men.

Sheriff Burke pointed toward the Burning Bullet Saloon. The saloon stood up the street off to the right. "That's the worst one," he told Vince, and then checked his rifle. "A fella by the name of Zachery Mills runs the saloon. Mills should be hanging at the end of a rope by now. Knew he was bad the day he rode into Durango."

Vince eyed the saloon for a minute. He counted the horses tied up outside and then checked on his own horse. Sheriff Burke had filled the watering trough that sat in front of the jail. Vince's horse was taking a drink. Vince patted the horse's back and then walked back to Sheriff Burke.

As he did, a man came staggering out of the shadows. "He... took my money! That no good bad egg... He took my money!" Frank Colby spouted off while staggering toward Sheriff Burke.

The first thing Vince noticed was the gun Frank Colby was holding. "Gun—"

Before Vince could warn Sheriff Burke about the gun, Frank Colby lifted his gun into the air and fired. "He took my money... that chiseler! Now the wife is gonna put me in the bone orchard!"

Frank fired at random, in a blind rage, with no intended target in sight. He thought he fired his gun up into the air. When he saw Sheriff Burke drop his rifle and hit the ground, his drunken face formed a confused question mark. "Bag of nails—"

Before Frank could finish speaking, Vince rushed forward. He knocked Frank over the back of the head with his gun. Frank's eyes rolled back into his head. He hit the ground. Vince ran to Sheriff Burke.

"My... stomach... Gut shot..." Sheriff Burke moaned in pain. "Gotta go find Doc Cunningham... He lives above his medical office..."

Sheriff Burke was bleeding badly. Vince ran off into the night as the lightning in the distance chased his thoughts. Ed and Dan stepped outside the Burning Bullet Saloon to see who had been shooting. They spotted Vince running off to find a doctor.

Both men were too drunk to even see straight, let alone cause trouble. All they could do was stumble back into the saloon while the other men standing outside just went about their business of drinking. So what if the sheriff had been shot? It wasn't any of their mind to interfere.

Vince found Doc Cunningham's medical office. He began banging on a door that held a square pane of glass in the middle.

Soon, a match came to life inside the medical office. The light brought a lamp to life. "Comin'... comin'..." a grumpy voice hollered. Doc Cunningham rubbed a half-shaven face with gray stubble as he moseyed through a hot room holding an old lamp.

When he opened the door and spotted Vince, Doc Cunningham said, "Yes?"

"Sheriff Burke is shot. Took a bullet to the gut." Vince spoke in a hard voice.

Doc Cunningham groaned. "Bring him here," he ordered. "Hurry." Doc Cunningham slapped on a gray hat and rushed past Vince. "I'm going to need help. I'll be back." Doc Cunningham hurried away to wake up Victoria Lodge. Victoria assisted Doc Cunningham. The woman had worked as a nurse for the Union Army during the War Between the States. She was used to blood and death.

Vince knew he had a hard job ahead of him. Moving Sheriff Burke wasn't going to be easy. The distance between the jail and Doc Cunningham's medical office was a good walk. No matter. Sheriff Burke had to be moved. Vince ran back to the wounded man. "Gonna lift you up onto my horse—"

"Can... mount... Help me walk..." Sheriff Burke pleaded as he cradled his stomach. Blood spilled through his fingers.

Vince fought to get Sheriff Burke onto his feet. The man leaned into Vince and nearly fell back down. "Easy... I'll drag you if I have to..." Vince nearly did have to drag Sheriff Burke to the medical office.

Sheriff Burke gritted his teeth in pain with each step he took, leaving a trail of blood on the hard dirt as he walked. Not a single man standing outside offered any assistance.

"Get him in," Doc Cunningham ordered as soon as Vince arrived. "Back room. Get him onto the table back there. Have to get that bullet out!" One look at Sheriff Burke was all Doc Cunningham needed. The man was bleeding something awful.

Vince spotted Doc Cunningham, standing at a deep sink, scrubbing his hands and arms with some sort of soap. A beautiful redheaded woman with the sharpest blue eyes Vince had ever seen was cutting up strips of cloth. Victoria glanced at Vince. She had seen his kind before. "Who shot him?"

"Frank Colby... He's whiskeyed up... Started firing his gun... Didn't mean to shoot me..." Sheriff Burke answered as Vince dragged him into a small back room that felt hot enough to melt iron. He helped Sheriff Burke up onto what Vince knew was an operating table and then hurried to open a closed back door to let the night air in. "Go... get Colby... Lock him up."

Vince nodded. Without saying a word, he maneuvered back outside and walked to the jail. Frank was still spilled like a sack of rotten potatoes. Vince took the man's guns.

Hoisting Frank up was going to be a job. Vince scanned the scene. No man standing outside seemed interested in them. Vince took his eyes to the eastern sky. The storm was growing closer. "Yeah..."

Vince hoisted Frank over his right shoulder. He carried the man into the jail and locked him in a holding cell, and then went back outside and grabbed Sheriff Burke's rifle. The eastern sky was still on fire with lightning, but none of the men standing outside seemed to care.

Vince decided Frank Colby wasn't important enough for anybody to come for him with a gun. He walked back to Doc Cunningham's medical office and waited.

Sheriff Burke was going to be out of duty if he lived. Vince knew what that meant. He was going to have to take over as sheriff. Was he willing to do that? With nothing else to do but wait, Vince found a chair and sat down.

Two hours later, Doc Cunningham walked out of the back room with his hands stained with blood. Victoria followed him, wiping her hands on a brown apron. Vince stood up.

Doc Cunningham walked past him to the sink. "He's gonna live." He spoke in a tired voice. "Good Lord was merciful."

"He's sleeping," Victoria told Vince.

"Best go tell his wife," Doc Cunningham told Vince. "She lives just outside of town."

"I'll go wake her," Victoria told Doc Cunningham. "Better Maye hears from me than a stranger."

Doc Cunningham didn't argue, and Victoria eyed Vince and then left. "She's a good woman," Doc Cunningham sighed as he washed blood off his hands. "Served as a nurse during the war. Came out here to escape her nightmares."

"Yeah..."

Doc Cunningham tossed a wary eye at Vince. "Seen your kind around. All dressed in black. Guns ready to kill. Eyes holding no soul or conscience."

Vince didn't reply.

Doc Cunningham went back to washing his hands. "You gonna take over being sheriff?"

"Reckon I don't have a choice."

"Reckon you don't." Doc Cunningham reached for a towel to dry off his hands. As he did, his eyes watched water stained with blood fall into a dark hole. "When will the killing stop?" he whispered.

"What?" Vince asked.

"Nothing." Doc Cunningham turned to face Vince. "You best be moving on. Nothing you can do tonight. I'll be keeping Sheriff Burke here for a day or so to watch him. Infection is always a danger."

Vince hated the way Doc Cunningham was looking at him. He walked outside feeling like a worthless trail snake. With nothing to do but go back to the jail, he got moving. It didn't take long to see that a strange horse was tied up in front of the jail.

Vince walked up to the horse. "Expensive saddle..." He ran his right hand over a saddle that most men would kill for. The initials AL were branded onto the sides of it.

Vince knew who was waiting for him in the jail. He checked

the eastern sky and then made his way inside. Lattimere was standing near the rifle rack. He eyed Vince the way a rattler eyes a loaded gun before striking. Vince walked to the desk and sat down. "Frank Colby is under arrest."

"I'm not here for Frank Colby." Lattimere towered over Vince by at least a foot—and Vince was a tall man himself. Still, the sight of Vince made Lattimere feel threatened.

Vince looked at Lattimere. Yeah, the man looked menacing. Cruel. Vicious. So what? Vince had tangled with worse during the war. As much as he hated to admit it, many of the Union soldiers he fought with were brave souls who had learned how to kill.

In battle, even the weakest man became a raging bull. Wounded animals struck hard in order to remain alive. What concerned Vince was Lattimere's eyes. Lattimere was a thinker, a schemer. He was the type of man who knew what he wanted and wouldn't stop until he got it—one way or the other. "Why are you here, Lattimere?" Vince asked.

"You know who I am. Good." Lattimere approached the desk, deliberately showing off a fancy gun belt that held two hungry Colt single-action Army revolvers that Vince knew were at least ten years old. "See you looking at my guns. I was an officer with the Union Army."

"Thought so by the way you talk. New York?"

"That's right." Lattimere kept his eyes on Vince. "War is over."

"Not some wars," Vince replied. "Folks don't like being forced to pay money to the likes of you, Lattimere."

Lattimere's eyes narrowed. "I came here to press charges against you for killing Gary Cappes. Word got to me that the two men who were with Cappes decided to get whiskeyed up instead of talking to the sheriff like I ordered. Heard the sheriff was shot."

"I'm acting sheriff now."

Lattimere scowled. Trying to get an acting sheriff hanged was going to be impossible. "Ride on, Vince," he warned. "This is my land. No one is going to stand in my way."

"Except me."

Lattimere's right hand formed a hard fist. "We'll see," he hissed, and then walked out into the night.

Vince stood up and made his way to the door. He watched Lattimere mount up and ride out of town. "Yeah... we'll see."

During the night, a hard storm arrived that followed the sun up. Vince managed to get a few winks of sleep and then decided to check on Sheriff Burke.

Sheriff Burke was still asleep.

"Tell him I'll be in Animas for the day. I'm having the hotel bring Frank Colby some supper. He's still sleeping off his whiskey. He won't be up for a while," Vince told Doc Cunningham.

Doc Cunningham just nodded.

Vince left Durango before Ed and Dan could. Both men were sleeping off their whiskey. The ride to Animas was tedious and wet, but uneventful. Vince had time to think about Lattimere on the trail.

What was Lattimere's plan? Was Lattimere after the railroad? No. The railroad would cut Lattimere down. That much was certain.

Was Lattimere trying to hold off land that the railroad wanted to buy? Maybe. But why bully innocent ranchers and store owners? If Lattimere wanted land, he would just try to run people off. Why demand protection money?

Miles had told Vince that Lattimere's ranch was running a good herd. The man didn't seem to be in a pinch for money, especially if he had enough money to hire guns.

Vince rode into Animas, which was smaller than Durango.

Even though Animas was only two miles north of Durango, running a straight line, the trail between the towns formed loops and curves in order to get around difficult passes. Ten miles' worth of trail divided the two towns.

On foot, a man could walk between Animas and Durango in an hour or so if he was bound to do so, but doing so would require a great deal of know-how. The river running to the west of Animas was treacherous. The landscape was rocky and filled with sharp rises that were nearly impossible to climb over.

Animas, Vince knew, might as well have been sitting a hundred miles out in the middle of an empty prairie.

A single street lined with poor stores on each side greeted Vince. Vince rode into town, drenched to the bone. No matter. He had work to do. Vince tied up his horse in front of the general store and walked inside.

A man with a thick mustache was standing behind a wooden counter writing something down on a piece of paper. "Help you?"

Vince walked up to the counter. He made his badge clear. "Wondering if you might be able to talk to me a bit about Art Lattimere?" he asked.

Peter Hauls quickly turned his back to Vince and pretended to focus on a shelf full of dry goods. "Ain't got no reason to talk about Art Lattimere. Best be moving on unless you want to buy something." The tone in Peter's voice sent Vince back out into the rain.

"Scared... yeah..." Vince studied the rain and then made his way down a muddy street to a rundown livery stable. He passed no one. The livery was closed. It seemed only the general store was open for business. Vince studied the saturated town for a while, memorizing each building, and then mounted up. "Time to go see Miles."

Peter watched Vince ride out of town with nervous eyes.

"Miles should have made you ride on! You're going to get us all killed." Peter slapped on a hat and coat and hurried out to a wet horse. He had to go see Jim Horton.

* * *

Vince rode east until he came upon Miles's ranch. He spotted the burned barn. Miles was standing next to the ruined structure, holding a rifle—but not in an alarming way.

No, Miles was leaning against his rifle, using the rifle as a sort of crutch, looking plum defeated. Vince rode up to Miles through the rain.

Miles didn't look up at him. "Went to check on the few head of cattle I have. Dead." Miles spoke as he stared at the black, burned mess of rubble.

"Shot?"

Miles shook his head. "Poisoned... at least that's the way it looks to me." Rain dripped down Miles's defeated face. "My wife is demanding we move on. Ain't got no more cattle and ain't got no money to buy any cattle."

Vince took his eyes off the rain. Lattimere had killed off Miles's cattle. Burned the man's barn down. Sheriff Burke was shot. Folks were scared. Lattimere had the reins. Vince wasn't sure what to do.

He could kill Lattimere... and hang for doing so. No, Vince had to draw Lattimere into a clean fight. Only Lattimere wasn't going to fall for that trap. Vince knew that. His gut knew that. "I've got a few dollars—"

"Save your money, Vince. Lattimere has won. I best take my family and move on."

Vince looked down at Miles, who continued to lean on his rifle. "Lattimere might not let you move on," he warned.

"Reckon I'm going to find out." Miles still didn't look up at

Vince. He was lost in thought, trapped in a mental prison filled with rusted chains holding his heart captive.

Vince heard movement. He looked toward the ranch house. Logan and Jonas Harter were out on the front porch, staring at their pa. For two boys to see their pa looking so defeated... Well, Vince knew. He had seen his own defeated once. That's when Vince lied about his age and entered the war, hungry for blood.

"Inside," Lauretta called out from inside the ranch house. Logan and Jonas obeyed.

Vince looked back down at Miles.

Miles didn't move.

"Lattimere," he whispered with blood in his voice—dark blood flooding up from cursed graves, blood that wanted to snatch the badge Vince was wearing off and throw it down into the mud.

Chapter Four

Vince regretted leaving Miles and his family. He had to ride back to Durango. With Sheriff Burke shot, Vince was required to stay in Durango unless he was out on business.

Staying at Miles's ranch wasn't a matter of life or death, not yet. Besides, Vince wanted to check on Sheriff Burke and then have a talk with the man's shooter. The trail back to Durango was wet and long.

Night arrived on the trail. Would Lattimere try to ambush Vince? Maybe. He was ready. He rode steadily in the saddle, ears and eyes alert, rifle in hand. As a man who had fought in the War Between the States—a man who had spent many nights sneaking into enemy camps simply to kill—Vince was more at home in the dark than he was in the light.

Halfway to Durango, Vince brought his horse to a stop at a bend in the trail. He got off his horse and moseyed down to a wild river filled with violent currents from the recent storm.

Vince bent low, placing his rifle across his knees, and thrust his hands into the river like a man thrusting his hands into a deep grave. Vince left his hands submerged for a few minutes, feeling the violent rush of the currents. "Yeah..." he grunted, images of blood-soaked faces attached to dead men tormenting his mind.

Vince finally brought his hands up out of the river. Nothing could wash away the invisible blood staining his hands. He wet his face and then stood up. As he did, the sound of a breaking stick hissed across the night winds. Vince remained still. "You should be home with your family."

Miles carefully made his way down a muddy embankment, careful not to slip. His lame leg ached and moaned, but that was okay. Miles was a tough bull. He walked up to Vince. "Wife wanted me to give you this." Miles held out a red and brown handkerchief. "Cornbread. Feared you might be hungry."

"You didn't ride this far to give me grub."

"No. I didn't." Miles lowered the handkerchief full of corn-bread. He scanned the river. "Nice this time of night. Peaceful. Always like the way the river sounds, too." Miles found a rock and sat down. Vince waited. "I ain't packing up. I ain't gonna let the likes of Lattimere run me off."

"Figured you wouldn't."

Miles grew silent for a few minutes. "It's gonna get bloody, ain't it?" he finally asked.

"Lattimere ain't the type of snake to die without striking as hard as he can."

"That no good bottom-feeder needs to be shot," Miles grunted.

"Yeah..." Vince leaned back against a hard tree that was curled up close to the river. "You thinking of doing that?"

"You bet I am... only..." Miles kicked at the ground with his good foot. "I couldn't get ten yards from Lattimere without getting myself shot by his hired guns. Reckon I could hide off someplace and plug him with my rifle... but then I might face the end of a rope."

Vince was relieved to hear that Miles was levelheaded and not the type of man to ride wild in his saddle. "Let me handle Lattimere. If I push him hard enough, he'll strike."

"Lattimere ain't gonna go against a badge, Vince. He'll strike at the helpless first."

Vince understood Miles's concern. Lattimere had poisoned the few heads of cattle Miles had left to his name. Now Miles had no barn and no cattle. What would be next? The man's two sons? His wife? "Miles—"

Miles eased up. "Reckon I best get back," he cut Vince off. He put the handkerchief holding cornbread down on the rock he had been sitting on. "I met Pater Hauls on the trail. He's calling for a meeting tomorrow. Said Jim Horton wants every fella who can ride to be at the meeting."

"Where's the meeting?"

"At Jim's ranch," Miles answered. "Jim used to have a nice spread... until Lattimere rode in. Anyway, my gut is telling me those two fellas will be chewing some hard rocks at the meeting."

"Rocks with my name on it."

"Yeah." Miles nodded. His eyes flitted around. A half-moon was slipping out from behind a canyon of gray clouds. The night sky was filled with ominous graves. Miles turned to face Vince. "I can tell you right now those fellas are going to demand you stay out of Animas and leave Lattimere be."

"What about you?" Vince asked as he leaned away from the tree his back was resting on.

Miles stared at Vince, his clothes damp from the night air, his stomach hungry from only eating a few scraps of beans and a slice of cornbread. "I ain't sure what to do, Vince. My two boys looked me in the eye after you rode off and asked me if I was going to turn yellow."

Vince stood still. Being called yellow by your boys was worse than being plugged full of bullets by a filthy drunk.

"I worked hard to build my ranch. My ranch ain't much, but it's all I got... all I got to give my boys. I can build another barn and buy more cattle, but I can't replace my sons. Lattimere might..." Miles stopped talking. He shook his head.

"But if you ride off, you won't ever be able to face your sons again. Right?"

"Right." Miles let out a tormented groan that caused Vince to lower his eyes. "Reckon I'll play the fool tomorrow. I'll act like I want you gone, but... you just ride smart. I'll play the fool and pretend I'm backing down like a coward. But you best know, if Lattimere comes for my boys or my wife, there will be blood."

"There's gonna be blood no matter what." Vince walked to Miles. He put a firm hand on the man's shoulder. "Best be riding back."

Miles nodded and moved back up the muddy embankment without saying another word, the wound of the violent river following him like a blazing fire. Vince felt sorry for the man. He was coming to respect Miles a great deal. Miles was the type of fella a man like Vince could depend on and call a friend.

Vince waited until he heard Miles ride off and then walked back to his own horse. He mounted up and rode on to Durango. He found Sheriff Burke resting well enough. The man was running a worrisome fever, but Doc Cunningham was keeping the fever under control with the help of Victoria.

"Where have you been?" Sheriff Burke asked as sweat ran down his pale face. His words came out broken and spilled.

"Animas," Vince answered. He glanced at Victoria, who was standing at a table, soaking ripped rags into a white pan filled with cold water. She looked at Vince but didn't speak a word.

47

"Doc Cunningham said my fever should break soon," Sheriff Burke told Vince. "You need to stay in town. Leave Lattimere be... for now." Sheriff Burke winced in pain.

"You best leave," Victoria told Vince.

Vince watched Victoria remove a rag from Sheriff Burke's forehead. She replaced the warm rag with a cold one. "I saw Art Lattimere's horse in front of the Burning Bullet Saloon. Rode in about three hours ago."

A question mark formed in Vince's mind. Why did Victoria tell him she had seen Lattimere ride into Durango? "Appreciate it."

"Don't," Victoria scolded Vince. "I know your kind. I also know Lattimere's kind. The decent people in this part of the land won't have peace until the likes of Lattimere are dead." Victoria turned to face Vince. She motioned around a hot, dry room that felt more like a prison cell than a medical station. "Back in Boston, a room like this would be condemned. Out here in this part of the land, people don't have nothing more. They fight for scraps... work hard... live hard, and yes... die hard. It's not right that a dog like Lattimere should take away what little they have."

Vince stared into Victoria's fiery eyes. "I know."

"Yes, I know you probably do," Victoria nearly spat at Vince. "You know only because you're being haunted by all the killing you've done. You're trying to make right for the blood you spilled. At least you seem to have a conscience. But that doesn't make you a saint. You'll never be able to ride fast enough to escape the men you killed."

"I reckon not." Vince walked to the room's door. He put on his black hat as he did, hiding his dark eyes.

"What's one more kill?" Victoria called out.

"Ms. Lodge... no," Sheriff Burke tried to scold Victoria.

"No?" Victoria swung around to face Sheriff Burke. "As long as Lattimere lives, this room will always have blood in it!"

Vince refused to turn and look at Veronica. He excused himself and walked back to the jail. He wanted to talk to Frank Colby.

Frank Colby was now stone sober, sitting scared and shaky on a stiff cot. When he saw Vince walk into the back area with the cells, he jumped to his feet, smelling like a rotted turnip drenched in sour whiskey. "Where ya been? Huh? I was nearly killed!"

"Nearly killed?" Vince asked without showing much concern. Frank Colby was nothing but a waste of air who spent his time drinking whiskey.

"Lattimere!" Frank wrapped his dirty hands around two rusted iron bars. "Lattimere threatened me! Told me to keep my tongue cold or I would eat a hot bullet!"

"I locked the jail before I left."

Frank pointed to a small window covered with iron bars. "There! Lattimere talked to me through them bars!"

Vince eyed the window. "You got some wrong doings with Lattimere?"

"Lattimere hired me on as a ranch hand. Fired me cause I... well, I kept getting all whiskeyed up. Reckon he had the right to fire me... but that don't mean he had the right to threaten me!" Frank hollered.

Vince reached into his coat and pulled out a red and brown handkerchief. "Here, eat."

"What... oh sure..." Frank grabbed the handkerchief from Vince. He unwrapped the handkerchief and, with greedy, hungry hands, snatched free a slice of cornbread. "What'cha gonna do about Lattimere threatening me, huh?"

Vince pulled up a wooden chair that was sitting against the back wall. He settled down. His back ached. He felt saddle sore.

Lattimere didn't threaten the likes of Frank Colby because the drunk knew how many heads of cattle he had. Some dangerous stuff was shooting around inside of Frank's head that concerned Lattimere. Lattimere could have killed Frank, but doing so would have caused the snake a good deal of trouble. "You don't like Lattimere, do you?" Vince folded two tired arms over his chest as he stared at Frank.

Frank gobbled down his cornbread, using both of his dirty hands to shove the cornbread into his mouth. "Can't say I do," he answered as bits of cornbread spilled from his mouth.

"What kind of work did you do for Lattimere?"

Frank ran a brown sleeve caked with weeks of trail dust across his mouth. "Lattimere hired me to do odd jobs... seeing how I ain't good at much. I can't ride that good and I can't shoot worth a flip. Tried to get on with the railroad. They wouldn't have me. Mr. Thurston said I smelled like a dead skunk drowning in a whiskey bottle... should have killed him for saying that about me."

"You ever get into Lattimere's ranch house?"

"Huh?" Frank threw his eyes at Vince. "Yeah, I did... started cooking Lattimere's meals after that fella with the funny eyes and funny voice quit on him."

"You can cook?"

"Not good, but I can round up some grub," Frank answered. "Wasn't Lattimere who put me in the kitchen. Dan Mufford put me in the kitchen. Dan and I go way back. Dan is meaner than a rattler, but he treats me good. Didn't want to see me sleeping behind a saloon."

"Yeah..." Vince thought for a minute. Frank's mouth was loose. That was good. "You shot Sheriff Burke. You could hang."

"What?" Frank nearly peeled out of his boots.

"Lattimere might want to see you hang, too," Vince pointed out.

"I ain't gonna hang!" Frank hollered. "I didn't mean to shoot Sheriff Burke, and you know it!" Frank grabbed the cell bars. His face grew pale. His eyes bulged. "Listen," he begged Vince, "I know I did wrong, but I ain't no killer. I have a hard time controlling my whiskey is all."

Vince shrugged his shoulders. "Seen men hanged while whiskeyed up."

Frank gulped. He had seen a man hang before. He had seen the man's horse ride out from under him and then seen the man's legs start kicking something violent as the shadows of fire came for his soul. All that was left was a pair of dirty boots swinging two feet above the ground. "Listen, I ain't—"

"How come Lattimere threatened you? You got some dirt on him?"

Frank's bulging eyes stared at Vince the way a wounded trail rabbit stared at a distant hole in the ground while being chased by a rattler. "All I did was read some papers! It wasn't my fault Lattimere left the papers on the breakfast table... I didn't mean to spill coffee on them!"

"Papers?"

"I took the papers to the kitchen and tried to clean them off the best I knew how," Frank blurted out. "My eyes got curious while I was cleaning the papers off, that's all."

"You can read?"

"Some... my ma taught me how to read the Good Book some..." Frank's eyes dropped. He felt dirtier than he looked.

"What did the papers you read say?"

Frank winced. "If I tell you—"

"You won't hang. You have my word."

"You'll protect me from Lattimere?"

"Yeah." Vince stood up. Frank 's putrid smell made Vince want to vomit. "Think on it. I'll be outside—"

"No... I'll talk," Frank yelled at Vince as he raised a pair of trembling hands up into the air. "Lattimere... he owns lots of land the railroad wanted. Railroad is paying Lattimere money to use his land. Lattimere wants to... oh... what did Dan call it when we were sitting in the saloon?" Frank had to think as his panicked mind raced wilder than a trail horse running from a snake. "That's it... Lattimere wants to be some sort of king... like over there in the old country. Lattimere wants to take over the railroad... build Animas up... take over Durango."

"Not possible."

"It is when Lattimere stole some bad papers belonging to one of the fellas who owns the railroad," Frank insisted. "I didn't read that, but Dan told me after I confessed, I read Lattimere's papers. Shortly after Lattimere fired me... I was real whiskeyed up anyway... never could stay sober."

"Yeah..." Vince studied Frank's eyes. The man was sober, sure enough. He was speaking hard truths that could get him killed. "Settle down for the night. Ain't nothing to be done until morning gets here."

"You gonna protect me from Lattimere?"

"Yeah."

"And make sure I don't hang?" Frank begged.

Vince took a few steps forward. "You best hear what I'm about to say and hear it right," he growled at Frank. "Sheriff Burke ain't likely to press any charges against you. When you get free, you best ride out of here as fast as your horse can take you and don't look back because there's gonna be blood shed— lots of blood shed. You best go find a place and sober up and get your mind right."

With those words, Vince walked outside to get some night air. He eyed the Burning Bullet Saloon. Lattimere was standing outside with Ed and Dan.

When Lattimere spotted Vince, he spoke a few words to Ed

and Dan then walked down the street to confront Vince. Vince rested his right hand on his gun.

"No need for that," Lattimere growled.

"What do you want?"

Lattimere smelled of whiskey—the good kind of whiskey, not the cheap yellow whiskey. "I want to warn you," he told Vince as Ed and Dan started down the street.

Vince narrowed his eyes and waited.

"You can't win against me. You're just digging your own grave. Best if you ride out."

"We'll see."

Lattimere raised a hand into the air once Ed and Dan drew close enough. "Frank Colby is in that jail."

Vince didn't respond.

"Frank worked for me. I want to pay for his legal counsel."

"What for?"

"I want Frank to come back to work for me. I should have never fired him," Lattimere answered. "Mr. Tames will be by tomorrow to talk to Frank. Judge Reed will be in town day after tomorrow. I want Frank to have a fair trial. Accidents... happen. No sense in Frank hanging... yet."

Lattimere's tone told Vince he had the power to kill or let a man live. Vince stared into Lattimere's shadowy face. "You best start digging your grave, Lattimere, because I ain't going nowhere."

"You rebels make me sick," Lattimere spat. "Fine. Drown in your own blood."

Vince took a step forward.

Ed and Dan went for their guns.

Vince had his gun drawn before either man could shoot. He aimed his gun straight at Lattimere's head. "Drop your guns and walk," Vince growled.

"You won't kill me," Lattimere spat again.

"If you ever go near Miles and his family again, I will hunt you down... So help me, I'll hunt you down and send you into the fire," Vince promised Lattimere. "If needed, I'll hang at the end of a rope." Vince kicked Lattimere back with a hard boot.

Lattimere stumbled into Ed and Dan. All three men crashed down onto the ground. Dan rolled away from Lattimere and tried to get a shot off. Vince put two bullets into his gun hand. Dan cried out in pain.

"Enough!" Lattimere roared. He crawled to his legs, dragging Ed up with him. Fearing that Vince might shoot him dead, Lattimere put his hands clear of his gun belt. "You're a dead man," he warned Vince. "I'm the master around here. You're going to learn that."

"You're a dead dog, Lattimere. Nothing more."

"We'll see!" Lattimere spat at Vince for the third time and then walked away sizzling like a hot bullet. "Ed, get Dan and come on. We're riding back to the ranch."

Ed dragged Dan up the street. Vince watched as Ed helped Dan mount his horse. Lattimere mounted his horse, yelled something vulgar, then stormed off into the night. Ed and Dan followed him like two whipped dogs.

"It ain't over, Lattimere," Vince promised.

A drunk man peeked his head out of the Burning Bullet Saloon. As soon as the coast was clear, he staggered down the street to the jail. "You the new sheriff?" the man asked in a drunk voice.

"Yeah."

"Name is Benny Ovens... no, Ovals..." Benny told Vince, fighting to stay on his feet. He pointed up the street. "I'm drunk up enough to tell you that Lattimere is filth... worse than cattle manure."

"I figured that."

"Reckon you did..." Benny stumbled into Vince, who did

his best to hold the man up. "My friend Frank is in the jail... Me and Frank go back a ways... We're partners with Dan Mill... no... Mufford. Dan ain't mean to us like some of the fellas are."

"Look, fella, go sleep—"

"Heard Lattimere talking in the saloon. He was sitting in the back with Ed and Dan... Heard what Lattimere was saying... You best want to hear what I got to say..." Benny staggered from side to side as he talked. He was a tall man, thinner than a piece of hay straw and just as pitiful as Frank.

Vince studied the street. A few men were standing outside, but not many. The two bullets Vince had put into Dan's firing hand had brought some outside.

Vince was sure Sheriff Burke, Doc Cunningham, and Victoria had all heard the shots. Victoria was nowhere in sight. "You best come into the jail."

"No..." Benny shook his head. He stumbled into Vince. "I ain't as dumb as Frank... drunk or not. We can talk when I'm sober. I don't want to die like this..." Benny pointed up the street. "Just send me on my way real rough like..."

Vince reckoned Benny would talk when he was good and ready. "Get on!" he yelled. "You ain't sleeping it off in my jail! Get!" Vince pushed Benny down and walked into the jail.

Three men laughed. "Looks like Benny ain't getting along with the new sheriff." One man didn't laugh, though. He eyed Benny with suspicion. He would ride out to Lattimere's ranch when no one was around and talk to Ed.

Benny managed to stand up and stagger up the street.

Inside the jail, Vince felt in his right coat pocket. Benny had slipped a piece of paper in there. "Meet me tomorrow behind the saloon at high noon."

Vince stared at the wrinkled piece of paper he was holding. Benny's handwriting looked like a two-year-old's, but the writing was legible. "Tomorrow at noon, huh? Okay. We'll see what comes of this."

Vince settled down for a long, hot night. When a little sleep finally managed to ride in, Vince dreamed of walking through a field of dead men. Each man reached up for him with bloody hands, screaming, "Join us! Join us!"

Vince startled awake just as the sun began to rise. Another day. More blood.

Chapter Five

Benny Ovals's body lay crumpled up like a bag of rotted potatoes. The shirt on his body stained with dry blood. His bare flesh ripped and torn with vicious knife wounds. Flies buzzed around the man's body like hungry vultures, dipping in and out in order to take a sour sip of rotted flesh the way a bumble bee sips sweet nectar.

The sound of the flies reminded Vince of scorched battlefields filled with dead soldiers. Vince had walked through many searching for a friend, slapping flies off the faces of dead men who were staring up at the sky through blank eyes.

Vince checked Benny's pockets. Nothing. An empty whiskey bottle rested next to the body. A wooden fence ran behind the buildings that shared the side of the street with the Burning Bullet Saloon. There were about ten yards between the buildings and the fence.

Mud was drying up from the storm the day before. The air was hot and punishing. Sweat was dripping down the sides of Vince's stone face. Whoever killed Benny did so when the morning air was cool.

Benny's body had been tossed behind the Burning Bullet Saloon. On purpose. Whoever killed him needed to make it look like Benny had been robbed and killed—separating Lattimere from the murder.

Vince knew Lattimere could have killed Benny anywhere. The body was left to mock Vince. Vince knew he had to take care of the body, but first he had business inside the saloon.

He checked his gun and walked through a wooden back door into a hot back room lined with empty card tables that would fill up by dark. A second door led out into the saloon.

Ed was sitting at a back table with a couple of trail snakes. Ed eyed Vince but didn't say anything as the man walked up to the wooden bar. The saloon wasn't impressive. The walls were bare. The tables run down. The air poisoned with the stink of old whiskey and quirleys.

A man who called himself Phil, the owner of the saloon, snarled at Vince, "I don't serve rebels."

"Didn't ask you to," Vince spoke in a hard voice.

Ed glanced at Phil. Phil went back to cleaning the inside of a whiskey glass. Surely Vince had come across Benny's body. Ed picked up a hand of poker cards and waited. Vince sat down on a hard stool.

Phil shot him a sour eye but didn't say another word. Vince eyed a dusty mirror that hung on the back wall behind the bar. He could see Ed and the fellas Ed was sitting with. Ed played a few hands of poker and then left the saloon.

"What's eating him?" David Spray asked as he reached for a glass of warm beer. David was on the short side but mean looking.

"He's run off to tell Lattimere something. What else?" Zachery Kitterman smirked as he chased down a hard drink of whiskey. It was clear the man was whiskeyed up. He wasn't much to look at drunk or sober. Just a dirty-looking ranch hand drifting toward his grave. "Speaking of Lattimere, I've gotta tell you something."

David tossed a careful eye toward Vince. He didn't work for Lattimere. Lattimere was a snake, and every man who had half a brain knew it. David owned a small ranch of his own but sold it off after his wife ran off.

He got on with the railroad but ended up getting fired after getting into a fight with another worker. Now David spent his days in the saloon and his nights passed out at the local hotel, earning a few pennies here and there working in the livery stable. "Lawman is in here."

Zachery looked at Vince. Vince didn't seem like much, and he was too drunk to care. "It's like this... I heard Lattimere telling Ed last night that he wanted Frank Colby dead. I saw Ed out behind the saloon earlier. He was wiping blood off his trail knife."

"Ain't none of my business what you saw, Zach."

"Yeah, I get that... man keeps his mouth shut. You hear too much mustard in these saloons, but not many fellas will die standin' up." Zachery's eyes rolled around in his head and then cleared. He leaned forward, almost falling out of his chair. "Lattimere fired me for no reason... that low-down varmint. Dave caught me sleeping out in the field—"

"Instead of mending a fence," David finished.

"Yeah, so I was drinking off a hard night. It's not like Lattimere is Johnathan O'Mally, the fella up in Oregon who has that bug spread. Lattimere is a snake..." Zachery struggled to make his eyes focus on David. "Look, Dave, the point is Lattimere wants Frank dead. I saw Benny giving that lawman sitting over there a hard time last night. Joe Daspers was with me. Joe rode off... my guess was to run his trap to Lattimere."

"Ain't none of my mind." David took down some more hot beer. Zachery was too drunk to play poker anymore. "I best be getting down to the livery stable. I'll be back tonight."

"Listen…" Zachery reached across the table and grabbed David's arm. David narrowed his eyes. "Dave, you best watch yourself. Lattimere's got blood in his eyes. That's all I'm saying."

"I don't know the fella. Don't intend to." David pulled his arm away from Zachery. "Go get something to eat and sleep it off."

Vince watched David leave the saloon. Zachery stood up and stumbled to the bar. He found a stool and sat down.

"I ain't serving you no more," Phil barked.

Zachery scowled but didn't put up a fuss. He turned his attention to Vince. "Lattimere wants Frank Colby dead. You best know that."

"Appreciate the tip."

Phil walked down the bar. He grabbed Zachery by his throat. "You best learn to keep your trap shut!" he yelled.

"Let him go," Vince warned.

Phil didn't let go of Zachery's throat. "Or what?"

Vince stood up. "I'm going to pull you outside and horse whip you."

Phil pushed Zachery away. Zachery stumbled backward and struck a table. He crashed over the table and hit the floor. "Your days are numbered, rebel."

"Are you turning yellow?" Vince asked.

Phil glared at Vince with murder in his eyes. "You ain't worth hanging over."

"You're just yellow."

Phil had heard Vince gunned down two vicious men. He wasn't about to go gun to gun with Vince. "Lattimere will deal with you."

"Like he dealt with the dead man outside?" Vince asked.

"What dead man?" Phil played the fool.

"Yeah…" Vince walked to Zachery. He pulled the man up. "You best come with me."

"If I was sober… you'd be dead," Zachery threatened Phil.

Vince pulled Zachery out into the bright sun. As he did, Victoria appeared in his vision, walking straight toward him. "Get to the jail and stay there if you want to live," Vince ordered Zachery. "You done crossed the line."

"Reckon… I did… Don't matter none, lawman." Zachery began to slur his words as he squinted his eyes against the bright sun. "The bottom of a whiskey bottle is my only home… my grave will be a mercy." Zachery pulled away from Vince and staggered across the street, nearly getting hit by a buggy pulling two older men who worked for the railroad.

Victoria walked up to Vince like a strong gust of wind. "Benny Ovals is missing. He's my cousin. I can't find him anywhere."

A heavy groan left Vince. He lowered his eyes. "Ma'am… you best come with me."

"You know where my cousin is?"

"Yeah…" Vince walked Victoria to the back alley on sorrowful legs. When Victoria came up on Benny's murdered body she covered her mouth. Tears began dripping from her eyes, falling down onto the green dress she was wearing. "He's been stabbed to death."

"I can see that…" Victoria couldn't take her eyes off Benny's body. "You were in the saloon—"

"Looking for answers. This man has been dead since early morning. I know who had him killed."

"Lattimere?"

Vince reached into his pants pocket. He pulled out the wrinkled piece of paper. "This man gave me this last night." Vince handed Victoria the paper.

Victoria immediately recognized Benny's handwriting. "He was killed..." she whispered.

"I ain't got no hard proof. The fella you saw me talking to out front said he saw one of Lattimere's men come out from behind here wiping blood off a trail knife." Vince removed his hat, revealing a sweaty sea of hair, and began shooing flies away from Benny's body. "I'll ask questions, but it ain't likely folks will talk, and no jury is gonna take the word of a drunk over Lattimere."

"Not in this town. No." Victoria wiped at her tears. "He was a drinker... but when he was sober, he was a gentleman. The whiskey took his soul."

"I best tend to the body, ma'am. Ain't no sense in leaving it out here to rot in the hot sun."

Victoria watched Vince swat at the flies with his hat. It was clear the man was upset. "His death angers you. Why?" she demanded. "Benny was only a drunk. Why should you care?"

"Reckon I've seen too many men die for nothing." Vince bowed his head. He had nothing more to say.

"I'll go talk to Mr. Haithers. He's the undertaker in this town."

Vince listened as Victoria walked off. There wasn't anything to do except tend to the body. He didn't know the gut of the law. What was he supposed to do with a dead man except have him buried? Doc Cunningham would only confirm the obvious. What could Sheriff Burke do? Not a blasted thing. Benny Ovals was dead. Soon his body would be tossed into a wooden box and buried under six feet of hot dirt. After that... nothing. Folks in Durango would go about their business. The saloons would still fill up. The sun would still rise and then go down. Benny Ovals would become a forgotten weed.

"Sorry you died the way I once killed a man..." Vince could only wait for the undertaker to arrive.

An older man with a gray beard and cold gray eyes that looked lifeless arrived and looked over the body. "Benny Ovals," Luke Haithers announced while folding a pair of scrawny arms over a fancy gray shirt. "Knew it was only a matter of time. It's only a matter of time before any man who steps foot into the Burning Bullet Saloon. Well, no matter, right, Victoria? We'd better get Benny fixed up and buried."

"How much will the burial cost me?" Victoria asked.

"I'll pay for the burial," Vince told Victoria.

"No, thank you," Victoria objected.

Luke stared at Vince as the man put his black hat on his head with a hand that had killed plenty of men. Death seemed to be following Vince. Luke had a way of knowing. "My usual fee, Victoria... but for you... and because I was fond of Benny... I'll knock off the charge."

"No charge?" Victoria asked in a surprised voice.

"You barely have any money as it is," Luke answered. "I can afford a wooden box for Benny. Besides..." Luke nodded toward Vince. "With this man around, I'm sure to get a lot of business. I've already buried two men he's brought into town."

"I best get to the jail. Ma'am." Vince excused himself and walked away. He wanted to talk to Zachery, who was leaning over the desk when Vince got back to his office. The man had passed out. "He'll be dead by night if I let him out." Vince took to the hard job of dragging Zachery back to the jail cells.

Frank watched as Vince pulled Zachery into a spare cell and threw the man down onto a hard cot. "What did Zach do?"

"Benny Ovals is dead" was all Vince replied.

"Dead? Benny? No!" Frank began pacing around his cell.

Vince left Frank to himself. The man stank. "He'll need some grub. Can't let him starve."

Vince locked up the jail and found some grub for Frank. After making sure the man ate, he visited Sheriff Burke.

"Dead?" Sheriff Burke asked. His fever had broken. Color was back in his face and life back in his eyes. He would live.

"Got a witness, but it ain't likely a jury is gonna believe a drunk."

"Are you kidding me? Zachery Kitterman would be laughed out of town if he said the sky was blue." Sheriff Burke was still in a good deal of pain, but he felt confident death had left his body. He couldn't sit up or roll over. It would take time to heal. "The body?"

"Undertaker is tending to it. Didn't see no reason to leave the body out in the sun."

"Victoria will be upset. She was Zachery's cousin."

"Yeah..." Vince glanced around the hot room Sheriff Burke was trapped in. "That yellow belly who owns the Burning Bullet Saloon will run his mouth to Lattimere. Saw him close the saloon and ride out of town when I went out to get Frank Colby some grub."

"Circuit judge will be in town tomorrow. I doubt Lattimere will do much before then."

"Lattimere wants Frank Colby dead. Frank has some dirt on him."

"What?"

Vince told Sheriff Burke what Frank had spilled to him the night before. "Frank ain't got no proof to back up his words."

"Maybe not, but Lattimere won't take any chances."

"Frank is scared stiff." Vince felt frustrated. The battlefield was drenched in blood and stained with the dead. Vince felt trapped and anxious to kill his enemy. "I'll be riding out of town for a bit."

"Figured you would."

"Jail is locked up. Reckon Lattimere can get in if he tries hard enough. Doubt he'll try, though. Lattimere won't risk more blood. Not now. He's playing his hand real smart."

"Too smart if you ask me." Sheriff Burke worried. "Lattimere is a hard killer. He won't stop until you're dead."

"Yeah..." Vince left Doc Cunningham's office. The sun was hot. The sky clear and blue. Durango felt like the inside of a sweaty barn. No man or woman who was prowling about seemed particularly interested in being outside.

"You!" a man yelled as Vince walked back to the jail.

Vince turned. A young man who didn't look old enough to shave rushed up to Vince wearing a brown suit and slicked-back black hair. "Yeah, what is it?"

"My name is Andrew Tames," the man proudly introduced himself. "I've just ridden back into town from seeing Art Lattimere." Andrew quickly brushed some trail dirt off his suit and then cleared his voice. "I wish to speak to Frank Colby."

Vince shook his head. "I'm riding out of town on business."

"I must insist—"

"You can insist until the dirt under your feet turns to water, boy. I've got business," Vince growled.

"When will I be able to... converse, if you will... with Frank Colby?"

"When I get back." Vince walked to his horse, and Andrew followed. "What now?"

"Judge Reed will be in town tomorrow. I need to speak to Frank Colby about his trial. I assume all the proper legal papers are in order?"

"I'll write up what happened." Vince checked to be sure his horse had taken down plenty of good water and eaten some grain. Riding in the heat would be slow. Pushing a horse too hard in the heat wasn't smart. Vince knew he wouldn't be back in Durango until late. He mounted up. "You're working for a snake, boy," he warned Andrew.

"I work for whoever pays me,' Andrew quipped. "If that

makes me look like a tyrant in your eyes, then so be it. I have a wife to feed."

"Yeah..." Vince rode off without saying another word. He needed to visit Miles.

While working his horse toward Miles's ranch, Vince came upon a man leaning against a tree. He was covered with blood. The man's horse was shot dead. A painful groan drifted into the air as Vince rode up. Vince jumped off his horse and ran to the man. "Take it easy, fella..."

"Name is... Jim Horton..." the injured man managed to speak as blood ran from his mouth. "Four men came up on me... beat me real bad... killed my horse..."

"Lattimere's men?"

Jim managed to look at Vince. "You Vince Dalby?"

"Yeah."

Anger flashed through the pain dripping from Jim's eyes. He had been beaten to within a mere inch of his life and then threatened. "I wish I could kill you... Look at what you're doing! Lattimere is blazing hot on account of you."

"Seems to me the men around here need to stand up and fight."

"Against hired guns?" Jim demanded, and then spit blood from his mouth. Vince could barely recognize the man's face. "Mister, the men around here live with sore backs from doing hard work all day. Understand?"

"Way I see it, if some farmers managed to fight off a strong army no less than a hundred years back, then the men around here can fight the likes of Lattimere. Truth is, the men around here are just plumb scared."

"Maybe we are... maybe we're scared for our wives and children!" Jim snapped. "You married?"

Vince didn't answer.

"You can just ride on..." Jim tried to move, but cried out in pain. He grabbed his ribs.

"I best get you into Durango to see Doc Cunningham."

"I can't afford to see no doctor."

Vince checked the trail. It was dry and clear, buzzing with taunting heat. Durango was a way off. Vince doubted Jim could make the ride, anyway. "How far is your ranch from here?"

"A good way. I was riding into Durango to find Miles. We went at each other's throats earlier. Miles seems to think like you do... Came to talk some sense into his head. He wasn't at his ranch. Figured he rode into Durango to talk to you."

Vince tensed up. Had Lattimere somehow gotten to Miles? "We best get you off the trail."

"Leave me be."

"No," Vince objected.

"You don't understand, do you? You're causing death to come to us. We can't fight Lattimere's guns. Lattimere even had a strong arm over the railroad for cryin' out loud! It's just best to pay him the money he wants. He leaves us alone when we pay him."

Vince squatted down. He looked into Jim's eyes. Jim was about Vince's age but looked much older. Strain, worry, and fear had taken their toll. "Judge Reed will be in Durango tomorrow. You can—"

"If we talk we die." Jim spit blood at Vince, which landed all over the front of the black shirt Vince was wearing. "What will a judge do, anyway? Judges in this territory are bought and paid for."

Vince figured Jim was right. "We best—" The sound of an approaching horse caused Vince to stand up.

Miles came around a bend in the trail. When Miles spotted Vince standing over Jim, he ran his horse forward. "Jim..." Miles struggled to climb off his horse. He hurried to Jim, dragging his bad leg behind him.

"Came looking for you. Lauretta told me she thought you rode into Durango," Jim managed to tell Miles as he spit more blood out of his mouth.

"Saw some of Lattimere's men on the trail. I headed into the trees and circled around back to the trail. Didn't see no sense in getting gunned down." Miles checked Jim's face as he talked. "Heard a rifle shot. I... figured someone had been gunned down. Stayed in the trees longer than I should have. Scared, I guess."

"We're all scared," Jim told Miles.

"I'm scared for my wife and boys," Miles told Jim. "My boys will ride hard and wild if something happens to me. Lauretta won't be able to rope them in. Logan already has bullets in his eyes. Jonas ain't far behind him. If Lattimere kills me, they'll go gunning for him."

"Then tell your friend to ride on!" Jim begged Miles. "Ain't no sense in that man causing trouble for us, Miles. You know that."

"What will it be?" Vince asked Miles. "If you tell me to ride on, I will. I won't look back. Ain't no sense in fighting with a bunch of cowards beside me."

"I ain't a coward," Miles growled at Vince.

"Then what will it be?"

Miles couldn't take his eyes off Jim's bloody face. The man was hurt and angry—and scared to death. Not for himself, but for his family. "Jim, if we don't stand up to Lattimere, he'll never stop. He's already burned my barn and killed my cattle. And look at you... When does it stop?"

"This is his fault—"

"No, Jim, this is our fault for not standing up to Lattimere sooner," Miles insisted in a shameful voice. "We're all so anxious to be above the snakes that we've turned yellow. No one wants to end up in the bone orchard. We don't draw out our shooting irons except to kill a trail snake or warn off a coyote."

"We're not killers, Miles," Jim pleaded as more blood spilled from his mouth. "Look at me... varmints who beat me had no souls. We have souls, Miles... We're not like them. We're God-fearing men."

"I know we're God-fearing men, Jim... but does God expect us to line up like dead cattle?" Miles turned to face Vince. "I ain't telling you to ride off. You're wearing a badge. You do what is right by the law."

"I don't think that fella will tell me who horse-whipped him."

"Leave it alone," Jim begged. "You're going to get us all killed!"

"I would rather die than live yellow in the eyes of my boys!" Miles yelled at Jim. "Lauretta is already demanding I pack up and ride out. She's scared worse than you are, Jim! And what am I doing? Belly-moaning is all while this fella here is doin' my fighting. No! I'm a man and I will die standing up!"

"Miles, you can't even walk good—"

"I had some time to think when I was up in the trees feeling mighty ashamed of myself, Jim." Miles pointed at Vince. "This fella here ain't no different from us. Only thing is he has the guts to fight and we don't. Well... from here on out, I ain't being yellow no more. You hear me!"

"You were never yellow, Miles. Your leg is hurt because you—"

"I was scared half to death the night I walked into the saloon..." Miles ran a hard hand across the back of his neck. "No more! I can't live being yellow... I can't leave with myself... can't look my boys in the eyes. Ain't right for a fella to burn down another fella's barn and kill his cattle. Just ain't right."

"You know Lattimere is connected to the railroad. This area will be full soon. Durango is growing—"

"And we keep paying Lattimere to let us work on our own ranches and stores, right?" Miles cut Jim off in an angry voice. "Don't you see, Jim? Lattimere is making us his slaves. He's already got his hands into the pockets of Durango. He has to be stopped... and I ain't gonna be yellow no more."

Vince nodded. "Let's get this fella to his ranch and then ride back to Durango. Looks like you're a deputy again."

"Never should have taken off my badge to start with."

Chapter Six

The hour was late. Vince asked Miles to check on Frank and Zachery after securing his horse at the livery stable. "Feed him good," Vince told an old man tending to the horses. He knew David Spray was at the Burning Bullet Saloon. Lattimere's horse wasn't in town. Neither was Ed's. Vince figured Lattimere was waiting for Judge Reed to show up before riding back into town.

"Your horse looks plum rugged. Shouldn't be riding him so hard." The old man fussed up a storm and then began grumbling to himself. "Man treats God's animals like nothing I've ever seen... maybe he should have a saddle put on him..."

Vince threw his saddle over a wooden saddle rest, grabbed his rifle, and walked out of the livery stable into a hot night. The town was dark. The only movement was in the saloons. The Burning Bullet seemed to be the favorite watering hole.

That was good. Vince knew where all the hard guns were drinking. The rest of the town knew better than to peek outside at night. Decent folks were indoors, resting after a hard day's work.

Miles was waiting outside the livery stable. He refused to put his horse up. "Might have to get back to the ranch," he told Miles before reaching town. "Best if I leave my horse ready to ride."

Vince studied a long street with careful eyes as he walked up to Miles. "Thought you were at the jail..."

"Saw some men go into Doc Cunningham's office," Miles informed Vince. "Gregory Bells and Winston Drakes."

"Railroad men?" Vince asked as he checked the rifle he was holding.

"No, but they carry money in their boots," Miles answered. "Winston Drakes is aiming to become governor if this territory is declared a state. Gregory Bells is his cousin. They're shadows. You don't see one without the other."

"Bells runs the banks?"

"You got it," Miles confirmed, keeping his voice low. "Gregory Bells wants Winston Drakes to become governor if'n the day comes. They're lower than trail snakes."

"Yeah..." Vince stopped, checking his rifle. "Anything wrong at the jail?"

"Besides Frank Colby smelling like a dead rat... nah. Zach is putting up a fuss over Frank's stink, is all. Wouldn't hurt if we can find them some grub."

"Grub can wait. Get back to the jail."

"Sure." Miles walked his eyes toward the Burning Bullet Saloon. "Don't see no horses that worry me."

"Not yet." Vince walked off with his rifle, ready to fight. He reached Doc Cunningham's office without finding trouble. Before he could open the door and walk inside, Victoria stepped out. "Ma'am."

"You got trouble," Victoria whispered. She glanced over her shoulder and then walked away without saying another word.

Vince watched Victoria make her way to the hotel and go inside. He felt sorry for the woman. There was no happiness in

Victoria's heart. Only anger, regret, and bitterness, three enemies Vince knew well. Vince stood still for a minute, feeling the heat of the night clawing at his stone face.

Would killing Lattimere absolve his conscience from bloody killings? No. Vince knew the bullet in his heart was fatal. He raised his eyes to a clear night sky filled with stars and then walked inside.

"You have to get that man out or else," Vince heard Winston Drakes demand as he walked into the room Sheriff Burke was resting in.

Two men in their late fifties were standing beside the bed Sheriff Burke was perched on. Both men, dressed in fancy suits and well groomed, reminded Vince of fat snakes feeding off dead corpses.

He couldn't tell the two men apart from each other, other than Winston Drakes had a neatly trimmed gray beard and Gregory Bells was carrying a thin gray mustache. Vince leaned his rifle against the front wall and folded his arms together without saying a word.

Sheriff Burke looked pale again, but he was managing to lean up on his right elbow. "Is there trouble?" he asked Vince, speaking in a voice that sounded strained and weak.

"Not yet," Vince answered. "Got Miles back with me. Found a man beaten on the trail today."

"A dead body and a beaten man..." Sheriff Burke leaned down and rested his head on a pillow.

Winston Drakes cleared his voice. "Any leads on the man who killed Benny Ovals?" he asked.

"Depends."

"On what?" Gregory Bells spoke up.

Vince kept his eyes low. "Depends if Lattimere is paying your salary," he answered.

"Now hear this!" Winston roared. "Sheriff Burke is still the law in this town. You are only the acting—"

"As long as I'm wearing this badge, I'm the law." Vince cut Winston off. "A man was stabbed to death. A second man was found beaten half to death. I have two men locked up who say Lattimere is standing in the shadows, calling the shots."

"You are pushing at a law-abiding man who does not appreciate being bullied by your badge," Winston scolded Vince. "I have come here to demand Sheriff Burke dismiss you at once."

"Nothing doing," Sheriff Burke told Winston. "Vince is doing his job. If Lattimere is innocent, then so be it. If he's guilty, he'll answer to the law."

Gregory Bells raised a hand into the air before Winston could respond. "Mr. Dalby, you fought in the war, did you not? For the Confederate Army, if I'm not mistaken."

Vince didn't answer.

"A man like yourself has probably seen a great deal of killing. All we ask is that you don't bring your war to our fair town."

"Meaning?" Vince asked.

"Art Lattimere served your enemies. Perhaps you are carrying a grudge for that," Gregory answered like a slithery snake. "Sheriff Burke can fight to keep you on as acting sheriff, but if the town feels you are violating your duty by carrying out a personal grudge against a law-abiding citizen, then we can have you dismissed."

"Get out," Sheriff Burke ordered Gregory and Winston. "You two ain't no better than a dead trail snake. Lattimere has you bought and paid for."

"Sheriff Burke, we will be looking for a new sheriff." Gregory spoke in a sickening, calm voice. "A meeting will be called once Judge Reed leaves Durango."

"Listen to me... there are good people in Durango. I ain't going nowhere."

"Our position states otherwise." Gregory looked at Winston. "Let's go."

Winston followed Gregory out into the night. They eased between the hotel and a legal office. "Vince Dalby has to die," he told Gregory. "We have too much at stake. If anyone finds out the truth, we'll hang."

"Not likely. But I do agree Vince Dalby is a thorn in our side," Gregory agreed. He pulled a fancy cigar out from his jacket pocket. Winston fished out a match for the cigar. "Thank you."

"What's the plan?" Winston asked. "I can't risk staining my reputation. I have a good chance at beating out Routt if Grant takes our side."

"We'll talk with Lattimere. We'll leave the blood on his hands," Gregory answered as he lit his cigar. "We'll tell Lattimere a few lies that will get him riled up enough to go after Vince Dalby."

Winston glanced about. No one was around. What Winston didn't know was that Victoria had her hotel room window open, and she was sitting by the open window in the dark. "Lattimere has John Dalton in a corner. John Dalton wants Lattimere dead."

"John Dalton is a fool," Gregory smirked. "The railroad is going to be our fortune and power. It's only a matter of time before I replace Dalton. Once I replace him, I won't have any problem controlling the railroad. Stephen McQuire will not offer any resistance. Not with you being the governor."

"I realize that, but Dalton killed that saloon whore... Lattimere has the goods on him," Winston said. "Dalton is keeping the railroad in Lattimere's pocket for now. McQuire is blazing hot, but Dalton is protecting Lattimere's position."

"I know all of this." Gregory sounded annoyed. He puffed on his cigar in silence for a minute. "We are in a position to have Lattimere kill Vince Dalby. We'll make Lattimere hang for the killing and then work on destroying John Dalton. One step at a time. Our goal is the railroad. The San Juan Mountains are loaded with power... That power can lead us straight to Washington."

"If we don't hang first," Winston told Gregory. "We're helping John Dalton with Lattimere—"

"Only for the moment," Gregory hissed. "We must place our pawns very carefully. Now follow me."

Victoria watched Gregory and Winston walk out the alley. She quickly rushed back to Doc Cunningham's office. Vince was still present. "You've got trouble," she told Vince.

"Victoria?" Sheriff Burke asked in a concerned voice.

Victoria closed and locked the door to the room. She moved close to the Burke then motioned for Vince. "I was in my hotel room, sitting beside the window getting air. I heard two men walk into the alley. The two men were Gregory Bells and Winston Drakes..."

Vince and Sheriff Burke listened as Victoria talked. When she finished, Sheriff Burke gritted his teeth. "I knew Dalton was behind the killing of Emilia Hutchinson. I saw them together more times than I can count. Dalton is married... I always feared it would be only a matter of time before Miss Hutchinson put Dalton on the hot plate."

"It's my word against the word of two men who are highly respected in this town," Victoria told Sheriff Burke.

"Yeah..." Vince looked at Victoria. Victoria was drowning in worry... and anger. The woman had buried her cousin and then spent the evening tending to a wounded man. While trying to settle down before falling asleep, she heard two killers spreading venom into the night air. "You best stay here for tonight, ma'am."

"They won't mess with me," Victoria told Vince.

"Never can tell."

"Vince is right, Victoria," Sheriff Burke insisted. "There are eyes all over this town. Someone was bound to have seen you come back here."

Vince knew the hour was getting late. Winston and Gregory didn't want to visit Sheriff Burke while the front street was busy. They carried out threats under the shield of darkness. "I best be getting back to the jail. I'll be back later to check on you."

"Fine," Victoria agreed.

Vince grabbed his rifle and walked outside. Only the saloons showed any signs of life. He moved to the jail on slow legs, studying each building he passed, searching for hidden guns.

The men standing outside the saloons only eyed Vince as he walked past. Not a single man dared to run his mouth or go for his gun. Vince reached the jail without incident.

Miles was standing outside, holding his rifle. "Winston Drakes and Gregory Bells went into the Burning Bullet," he told Vince.

Before Vince could speak, rifle shots sliced through the night air from behind the jail. "Go that way and meet me around back!" Vince pointed to the right side of the jail and then took off running. He eased around a hot wall. The side of the jail was cloaked in darkness. Vince moved down the wall and stopped when he reached the end.

Was Miles in position? Vince couldn't wait to find out. He threw his head around the side wall and studied a dark ocean. Only dim light coming from a cell lantern flowed out through two small windows covered with bars. The bottom of the back wall was blacker than death.

Vince depended on his ears. He listened. Miles was making noise from the opposite wall. Not good. Whoever did the shooting would hear Miles. Vince didn't suppose the shooter was standing in the dark.

There was no back fence behind the jail, just open land leading into hill country. Vince was certain Lattimere had sent a man to kill Frank and Zachery.

Miles stood in place, peeking around a wooden wall, waiting. He couldn't see. But then he heard the sound of two horses tearing off into the night in the distance. "Vince!"

Vince heard the horses. They were too far away to ride after. There was no chance of catching up. Miles's horse was run ragged and needed to rest. Vince's own horse wasn't in any better shape. Vince moved to the back of the jail.

He lit a match as Miles joined him. Two wooden crates had been moved into place. Both crates were tall enough to let a fella aim a rifle through the small cell windows. Vince stepped up onto one of the crates, knowing exactly what he was going to see.

Frank and Zachery were both dead, sprawled out on the dirt floor. Whoever killed the two men filled their chests full of hot lead. Blood was streaming onto the floor. The blood of two men who, like Benny Ovals, would be buried and forgotten like sour weeds. "They're dead."

"Lattimere!" Miles squeezed the rifle he was holding.

"Didn't think Lattimere would strike like this. Thought he was waiting for Judge Reed." Vince gritted his teeth.

Lattimere had fooled him. Or was Lattimere behind the killings? Had Winston Drakes and Gregory Bells somehow set up the killings? Vince didn't know. All Vince knew was that, without Frank and Zachery, he didn't have a leg to stand on.

Vince stepped down from the wooden crate. "Let's tend to the bodies."

"Yeah... okay." Miles followed Vince into the jail, limping hard. He felt angry and trapped. "Acting outside the law is the only way we're going to kill Lattimere," he told Vince.

"No deal." Vince shook his head. With the help of Miles, he carried Frank's and Zachery's bodies around to the back of the jail. "Undertaker will take care of them tomorrow. Nothing we can do tonight."

"Did you notice no one came running when the shooting—" Miles began to ask as he grabbed the rifle he leaned against the back wall of the jail when a bullet exploded a mere inch from his head, striking the back wall of the jail.

Vince hit the ground and rolled to the side as a barrage of bullets began licking the ground next to him. He yanked out his gun with a lightning fast hand and began firing at a broken watering trough standing behind a building a few yards from the jail.

Vince's eyes were adjusted to the dark. He spotted three men firing from behind the watering trough. He was out in the open. Not good.

Miles crawled around to the side of the jail and began firing his rifle. "Take cover!" he yelled.

Vince cleared his gun and then crawled forward, staying low on his belly as Miles covered him. Miles kept the shooters held down as Vince managed to take cover. Once Vince was secure, he went for his second gun. "Keep shooting."

"Where are you—"

"Keep shooting!" Vince took off running for the front of the jail. He took a hard turn and ran onto the wooden walkway. He ran two buildings up and then dived back into the darkness, coming up on the back of a dark building.

He immediately spotted three men hunkered down behind a watering trough, firing rifles. Vince wasn't the type of man to shoot his enemy in the back. When Miles stopped to reload,

Vince ran forward like a silent owl, his gun hungry to kill. "Throw your rifles down!"

The three men firing at Miles were all startled. They turned around the way a kicked coyote swings around to bite his attacker.

Vince dropped down onto one knee and began firing his gun. One razor-sharp bullet after the next sliced through the hot night air, cutting through the darkness with vengeful cries. The three men who turned to kill Vince didn't stand a chance. Vince shot all three men dead, the way he would shoot a wild snake dead. "Miles!"

"On my way!" Miles moved forward when he saw Vince light a match. Vince was looming over three dead men dressed like filthy saloon hounds. One man was shot through the head. The second man had his chest cleaned out. The third man didn't have a face. "If the sky ain't blue..." was all Miles could manage to say.

"These fellas aren't Lattimere's hired guns," Vince told Miles as he reloaded his guns. "They rounded up together behind that watering trough. A trained gun knows to spread out."

"They smell of whiskey, too... That fella there is Nathan Edwards... and that's Willy Cooper... Can't say I know the other fella..." Miles was now holding a lit match, giving Vince light to reload his guns. When the match burned down, he threw it down. "You just shot them dead..."

"I've been in a lot of battles. Learned a lot of tactics," Vince explained without an ounce of pride or arrogance. He was just stating a fact. "When I saw those three fellas bunched up together, I knew they weren't Lattimere's men. Easy kills."

"Maybe for you," Miles whispered and then walked off, wondering just what kind of man Vince Dalby really was.

Vince put his guns away and then gathered up the three

rifles. "They didn't wait," he told himself, aiming his words at Winston Drakes and Gregory Bells. "Now I've got trouble with those snakes. Best to send Miles back to his family. It'll only be a matter of time before he ends up sleeping under the dirt."

Across the street, Winston and Gregory waited. When they saw Miles walk back to the jail and Vince follow a minute later, their faces dropped into a dark pit. "This isn't over," Gregory hissed. "Not by a long shot, Dalby. Not by a long shot."

Chapter Seven

Lattimere rode into Durango, sitting high in his saddle. Four men rode behind him. Ed was leading the way. Dan had been ordered to stay back at Lattimere's ranch. Frank and Zachery were dead. Lattimere had rid himself of two sharp thorns.

Judge Reed was a hard man. Lattimere wasn't certain if he could buy the judge or not. He wasn't up to taking any chances. Not with Vince on the prowl. Besides, Lattimere had sent a clear message to Vince that he was controlling the game.

Lattimere arrogantly brought his horse to a stop in front of the jail, where Andrew was outside speaking with Vince and Miles. "Heard the news. You run a lousy jail, Dalby. Maybe you would be better off shoveling horse manure." Lattimere cocked his head back and laughed. The men with him joined in. "Mr. Tames, join us in the saloon."

"I'm sorry, Mr. Lattimere. I can't at the moment. It seems my brother has gone missing," Andrew answered. "Last night was a bloody night. Five men were killed. Now my brother is missing. I fear the worst."

"Your brother works for the railroad." Lattimere's attitude turned serious.

"My brother offers his legal services for the railroad. Yes, you are right, Mr. Lattimere."

Vince watched a dark frown wash over Lattimere's murderous face. "Ed, stay in town. You men, follow me." Lattimere kicked his horse and headed out of town.

Ed eyed Vince and then rode up to the saloon.

"My brother was staying here in Durango," Andrew continued to talk to Vince and Miles. "He has some years on me... twelve to be exact... and far more experience. The railroad refused to hire me because I'm still a bit young and lack solid experience. My brother was taking me under his wing. I fear something has happened to him."

"Your brother is Arthur Tames, right?" Miles asked.

Andrew nodded. "Arthur came right over on the boat with our mother, straight from Ireland."

"Ah, yeah, that's how I know him. He talked funny."

"Our mother was Irish," Andrew explained impatiently. "Arthur and I have different fathers. That's all I'll reveal on a personal note. Now, I want you two gentlemen to go search for my brother."

Vince was mentally drained. He had barely had a wink of sleep. Setting out to search for a missing man would require a lot of riding. "Was your brother hungry for the bottle?"

"He was a sober man. I know that might sound like a lie, seeing how he was Irish, but may lightning strike me dead if I'm lying."

"Married?" Vince asked.

"Arthur's wife died of the fever some years back. He didn't have any children from the marriage." Andrew shook his head. "Arthur is a man of diligence. When his wife died, he threw

83

himself into his work. He was determined to train me up. Arthur isn't the type of man to wander off and vanish."

"Not likely after all the killing done last night." Miles looked at Vince. "We best saddle up."

"Any idea where your brother might have rode off to?" Vince asked Andrew.

Andrew placed two worried hands behind the brown suit he was wearing. The morning was blistering hot, but Andrew didn't seem affected by the heat, or at least he didn't show it. "My brother enjoyed taking sabbaticals to the river."

"Sabbaticals?" Miles asked. "What's that?"

A loud train whistle erupted into the air. "The ten o'clock is right on time, I see." Andrew looked to the north. A cloud of white steam appeared in the distance. He turned back to Miles. "Mr. Harter, my brother enjoyed sitting by the river is all I meant to imply."

"Oh..." Miles rubbed the back of his neck. "Sometimes I don't understand them fancy words you educated fellas use."

"What part of the river did your brother like to sit at?" Vince asked.

"Every part," Andrew answered in a helpless voice. "My brother could roam the banks of the river every day of the year. He said the river calmed his aching heart."

"Yeah..." Vince listened as a thundering locomotive soared into Durango. He didn't care for trains. "We best ride, Miles. We'll search the river for a few miles and see what we find."

"Hey... look there," Miles nodded toward the Burning Bullet Saloon. Winston and Gregory were now standing outside, talking to Ed.

"Yeah... let's ride."

"I should come with you," Andrew insisted.

"Rather you stay in town." Vince had no desire to make Andrew a marked target. The fella was young and green. He had a wife. There was no sense in nailing a grave to his forehead. "We'll be back before dark."

"Judge Reed will want to speak with you. He is going to convene court at two, sharp," Andrew informed Vince.

"Already spoke to Judge Reed after he rode in on the stagecoach."

"You did?" Andrew asked.

"About an hour ago," Vince confirmed. "Judge Reed won't be needing to talk to me anymore today." Vince walked off toward the livery stable without saying more. The ground beneath his boots rattled from the approaching train.

Miles fetched his horse and rode up to the livery stable. He waited for Vince while keeping his eyes on the saloon. Winston and Gregory had walked into the saloon with Ed. "Think he's dead?" Miles asked Vince after riding out of Durango about half a mile.

"Could be." Vince nodded. "We'll check the river for a bit, and then you ride on back to your ranch and see about your family."

"Will do."

Vince and Miles rode the trail until it curved away from a powerful river. They tied up their horses, collected their rifles, and walked down a slight embankment to the river. Vince had to admit the land was rough, but gorgeous. He could understand why people wanted to make Colorado home.

The river, although dangerous, was as free as a wild eagle. The land surrounding the river complemented the river in a way Vince figured some poet could describe. He sure couldn't. There was no need to. Words messed up a good ride.

"I'll walk down the river a bit," Miles told Vince.

"Okay." Vince started up the river, keeping to a narrow trail that time and rain had carved out. He walked about a quarter of a mile before finding empty bullet cartridges—four, to be exact. Vince bent down and picked up an empty cartridge. "Good bullet..."

The ground was disturbed. Some low-hanging branches were broken. Vince studied the scene. He studied the dirt.

About five feet from the spot where the empty bullet cartridges lay, Vince spotted dried blood. He examined the blood and then focused on the broken tree limbs. "He was walked down here... not dragged out."

"Vince!" Miles's voice carried up the river.

Vince leaned up. He spotted Miles waving at him from a curve in the trail. Vince picked up the remaining empty cartridges and walked to Miles. "What did you find?"

"Arthur's body... caught on some trees that fell across the river," Miles explained. "He's been shot in the back... looks to be about four shots from what I saw."

Vince showed Miles the empty cartridges he had found. "Spotted some dry blood on the ground."

"Hey, look at that... see those initials carved into the cartridges?"

"'Yeah. I saw. Lattimere's initials," Vince confirmed.

"Lattimere is known to carve his initials into his bullets." Miles looked at the river. The river was so loud he had to nearly yell to be heard. "Lattimere killed Arthur Tames."

"Looks that way." Vince looked about. The trail was about a hundred yards away. If an ambush occurred, Vince knew he and Miles could duck behind the trees, but then what? The river had them trapped. "We best go get the body—"

A bullet cut through the air. The bullet sliced the side of Vince's neck. Vince grabbed Miles and threw him down behind a tree instead of fretting over his wound. A shower of bullets began to rain down.

"You're hurt," Miles yelled out as Vince took cover by a tree nearby.

"I'll live!" Vince kept his back up against the tree as one hungry bullet after the next tried to find him. "I'm counting four shooters!" he called out to Miles.

"Yeah, four!" Miles confirmed. "We're tied down pretty good!"

Vince checked his rifle as blood streamed down his neck. He had suffered worse wounds in the past. "They're spread out pretty good!"

"What do we do?" Miles asked.

"Two of them will keep firing while the other two move around to get a good shot at us! You keep in that direction and I'll keep in this direction!" Vince pointed about with a quick hand. Miles nodded in agreement. He was scared half to death.

Dan wasn't firing a rifle. He was standing back while four hired guns kept Vince and Miles pinned down. "You had him in your sights!" he yelled at a man named Ryan Belts.

Ed rode up before Dan could kick dirt at Ryan. "What's going on?" Ed demanded as he ran to the tree Dan was standing behind.

"We got Dalby and Harter trapped down by the river."

"Lattimere give the order?" Ed asked. He studied the scene. Four armed men were standing behind trees, firing down at the river.

Dan shook his head. "Not Lattimere. Dalton."

"We don't work for Dalton!" Ed growled.

"We work for who pays the most, Ed! Dalton is tired of dealing with Lattimere. He's going to pin the murder of Arthur Tames on Lattimere and be done with it! You know Lattimere ain't gonna win against the railroad!"

Ed wasn't sure what to think. He knew Arthur Tames was the only fella keeping Lattimere roped up in a legal sense. Ed didn't know all the rabbit holes of the game. All he knew was Lattimere wanted Tames dead but dared not touch the man.

Sometimes, the mindset of Lattimere confused Ed. He would have killed off Tames before the moon grew full.

"You with us, Ed?" Dan asked. He held up his wounded gun hand. "Dalby is gonna pay! You best be with us and not against us..."

Ed didn't like being threatened. He grabbed Dan and pushed him toward the trail and away from the tree he was taking cover behind.

Vince was searching the trees with his rifle. When he saw Dan stumble out from behind a tree, he took aim and fired. A single rifle bullet tore through Dan's forehead.

All Ed saw was the back of the man's head burst open. He ducked down.

"He got Dan!" Ryan yelled out.

Ed looked at Dan's body. Dan was sprawled out on his back with his arms out as if he were preparing to hug something. Blood was pooling down his face. "Keep firing!" Ed ordered. He whipped out his gun and began firing down toward the river. "Joe... Ken... spread out to your right and left and start moving down... See if you can get a shot at them! Ryan and me will cover you!"

Vince heard Ed scream out an order. He had to act. There was no way to keep four armed trail snakes pinned down. Vince looked up at the tree he was taking cover behind.

"Yeah..." Without telling Miles what he was doing, Vince shoved his rifle down the back of his shirt and then began scurrying up the tree like a scalded squirrel. Miles spotted Vince climbing the tree but didn't call out.

When Vince got high enough, he situated himself on a sturdy tree limb and then used his right hand to pull his rifle free. His hands were covered with tree sap. Blood was still streaming down his neck. Vince had to take a second to clear the stinging sweat out of his eyes.

He was up high enough to see the trail. With careful balance, he could shoot down any man who came into his sights. The tree limb Vince was standing on was sturdy. A second tree limb hanging about waist height allowed Vince to lean just enough without falling.

Joe moved out from a secured position and began moving to his left while holding a rifle. The man was built like a bear and could fire accurately, but was slow on the draw.

Joe didn't have many brains. He killed only when he was paid to kill—and at times when a fella caused his temper to flare. He was a man who ran the land like a wild bull.

Vince spotted Joe in his sights. He took aim at the man and fired. A bullet ate through Joe's heart as his body thundered backward and crashed up against a tree.

Ken yelled out, "He got Joe!"

Vince followed Ken's voice. He was perched behind a tree about twenty yards from Joe. Vince spotted Ken's hands holding his rifle. He took aim and fired. Ken's firing hand erupted into a cloud of blood. He dropped his rifle and let out a painful howl.

"He got Ken!" Ryan hollered. "He's up yonder in the trees!" Ryan stopped firing and ran for his horse, exposing himself. Vince picked him off. A bullet ripped the back of Ryan's head open a few yards from his horse.

Ed knew Vince was firing from the trees. He threw down his gun and stepped clear with his hands held up in the air. "Dalby... I ain't armed!"

Miles caught sight of Ed. Yeah, Ed wasn't armed. Miles didn't care. He shot the man through his heart. Ed lunged backward and crashed up against his horse. The horse let out a fearful cry and took off running down the trail. "You threatened my family," Miles hissed. "Now you can rot in the fire!"

Vince checked the scene, then threw down his rifle. A

minute later, his boots touched solid ground. "Clean shot," he called out to Miles.

"He wasn't armed," Miles told Vince, checking his rifle.

"Looked armed to me."

Miles stared at Vince. He simply nodded. "I best go check on my family. Lattimere is gonna breathe fire over this."

"Wasn't Lattimere who ordered the ambush."

"Yeah, I get that, but Ed was one of his best men." Miles limped back up the trail. Vince followed. "You sure don't have a problem killing a fella," he told Vince while checking the dead bodies.

"Didn't see you having a problem killing that snake," Vince spat at Ed.

"Nope." Miles mounted his horse. "That dead snake threatened my family. Now he can rot in the fire. Call me yellow for the way I shot him down. Don't make no difference to me."

"You did what needed to be done." Vince walked up to Miles's horse. To Miles's shock, Vince extended his right hand. "Proud to call you a friend. I don't say that to no man. I'm saying it to you."

Miles felt right proud to shake Vince's hand. "Best be getting on. Need to check on my family. Before I go..." Miles pointed at the dead men. "Lattimere is losing a good bit of his stock. Dan and Ed were two of his best guns."

"The railroad has enough money to hire more guns. I doubt Lattimere was paying for his hired guns out of his own pocket."

"Runs deep, don't it?" Miles asked as he secured his rifle.

"Man's soul is a whisper of light and darkness that fails to seep over the mountain dawn."

"Huh?"

"Something a fella I knew in the war told me once. I was too young to understand. Now I think I do," Vince answered. "You best get to riding. I'll bring the body of Arthur Tames back to Durango."

"Reckoned you would. Appreciate it." Miles gave his horse a kick.

Vince stood back and watched Miles move on down the trail. "Yeah... be careful, my friend."

It took Vince longer than expected to get the body of Arthur Tames roped down onto a horse belonging to one of the dead men. After Arthur's body was properly tended to, Vince threw the dead bodies dirtying up the ground onto the remaining horses.

He put Dan and Ed's body onto the same horse. After tying all the horses together and stationing them out into a line, Vince got moving.

What would people think when the acting sheriff rode in with six dead men? Vince figured Winston and Gregory would use the situation to call some sort of meeting.

Judge Reed was in Durango. That's all that mattered. He was the man Vince needed to chew the fat with. Vince settled on his saddle and kept his horse moving. "Gonna make sure you get plenty of good oats," he promised his horse. "You've been a mighty good friend."

Victoria had just stepped out of the hotel when she saw Vince stop a line of horses in front of the jail. Men and women, on horse or on foot, all stopped and stared. Some women gasped in fright, while some of the men could only shake their heads.

Victoria walked to Doc Cunningham's office and told Sheriff Burke what she saw. Sheriff Burke's wife was with him. The poor woman begged her husband to leave town. "He can't ride," Victoria warned.

"Keep your eyes open. Doc Cunningham is out on the O'Neil's ranch, tending to Mrs. O'Neil. He said she has a bad fever," Sheriff Burke ordered Victoria. "Stand clear of the jail."

"Vince Dalby just rode into town with six dead men." Victoria spoke in a worried but sour voice. "You know what that means."

"If Vince brought the bodies into town, that means he can handle himself. Best he remains alive than dead."

Victoria quickly checked Sheriff Burke over and then made her way back outside. She stood back and listened.

"Those are Lattimere's guys," a man rambled.

"Yep. I can see Ed's boots plain from here." Another man ran his mouth while smoking a quirley.

"That awful man is a menace," the wife of a well-to-do shop owner insisted. She huffed, brushed at her fancy dress, then moseyed off like she was queen of the world.

Vince spotted Victoria standing off in the distance with the onlookers. He secured each horse, then made his way toward Doc Cunningham's office.

"What happened?" a man called out. Vince didn't answer. "They try to bushwhack you?"

"You killed Dan Mufford and Ed Newman!" another man hollered. "Who do you think you are!" Vince had seen the man yelling at him while standing outside the Burning Bullet Saloon with Ed a few times. "Somebody should hang you!"

"Enough!" Victoria broke through the crowd. She rushed to Vince and pointed at his battle-worn clothes and bloody neck. "Look at him! Does it look like he just walked in from a picnic? And those men—" Victoria pointed toward the horses secured in front of the jail. "Who are they? Killers! Paid killers!"

"Ma'am, I can handle—" Vince began to try to silence Victoria.

"I'm going to speak my peace!" Victoria pointed around.

"You men... you all walk around deader than a condemned soul. You spend your time in the saloons drinking yourselves into the grave. You turn a blind eye to the likes of Lattimere while innocent people suffer! You're all cowards! Do you hear me? Cowards! At least this man"—Victoria pointed at Vince—"has the guts to fight!"

Vince touched his neck. He felt dry, caked blood. "Those fellas ambushed me and Miles Harter while we were down at the river searching for Arthur Tames. We found his body in the river. Someone filled him full of holes."

"What's going on here?" The voice of Andrew Tames cracked through the heat. He pushed his way through the crowd. One look at Vince caused the man to groan. "You found my brother..."

"At the jail. Put his horse away from the others," Vince explained.

Andrew threw his eyes past Vince. He immediately spotted his brother's body. "How?"

"He was shot and thrown into the river."

"Who?" Andrew yelled as he clenched his hands into two tight fists.

"I don't know." Vince saw tears swell up in Andrew's eyes. "I'm sorry," was all he could say.

"So am I!" Andrew pushed past Vince and ran to his brother.

As Andrew ran off, a tough old box of nails known as Judge Reed appeared. "Let's break this up. You heard me. This is the business of the law," he barked.

The angry crowd slowly broke apart. Some men drifted back to loaded wagons. Some men walked to the saloons. Some women drifted into the shops.

"What happened?" Judge Reed demanded as he soaked in Vince's appearance.

Vince explained the scene.

Judge Reed listened. "Looks like I won't be leaving Durango anytime soon," he told Vince.

Vince reached into his shirt pocket. He pulled out the empty cartridges he found at the river. "Here."

Judge Reed accepted the cartridges. The first thing he noticed were the carved initials. "Art Lattimere," he told Vince and then shook his head. "You can bring Lattimere in on questioning, but anyone could have stolen some bullets from him... and from what I've seen so far, I don't think I can get a jury that has enough guts to put a rope around Lattimere's neck."

"I need to check your neck," Victoria told Vince.

Vince nodded. "Mind if we eat at the hotel after I'm checked?" he asked Judge Reed.

"Don't mind at all." Judge Reed looked deeply into Vince's eyes. "I knew a Texas Ranger once. Hard man. Rode hard and killed hard after his wife and son were slaughtered. Helped clear out some of the most vile vermin there is, too."

"Judge Reed, I need to—"

Judge Reed held up a patient hand. "A man kills for different reasons. Can't say I agree with all the reasons. That's why I'm a judge. But I've learned that when a good man is broken before he can learn to ride right, he ends up riding with blood in his eyes until he dies. Doesn't have to be that way, though."

Vince thought of the word Miles's wife used. Absolution. "Reckon sometimes it's too late for a man to clear the blood out of his eyes."

"Tell that to the Texas Ranger I spoke of." Judge Reed's words let Vince know he was the Texas Ranger in question. "Came back to my home and found my wife and son gutted. Never seen anything so horrible in all my years. I set out to kill as much as I could... and I did my killing. When no man was riding with me, I hung vermin from tall trees without a fair trial. I lost my soul... eaten alive with fury."

Vince listened.

Judge Reed drew in a deep breath of dry, hot air. "Time came when I had to make my peace with God. I was on my way to the fire. My wife and son are with the angels above. Reckon that's where I want to be, too." Judge Reed finished in a tone that told Vince all he needed to know.

"I better check your neck," Victoria told Vince. The words Judge Reed spoke fired her angry heart.

"See you in a bit." Judge Reed walked off to console Andrew.

Vince followed Victoria into Doc Cunningham's office. She set out to clean his neck while he told Sheriff Burke what happened. "Lattimere will be burning hot," Vince warned Sheriff Burke. "I killed his best guns. The railroad will hire more. John Dalton ordered the ambush."

"It's your word against a man who has a lot of power under his gun belt," Sheriff Burke told Vince in a strained voice. "Lattimere and the railroad will both want you dead now. You best ride out as fast as you can."

"I ain't taking off this badge." Vince moved his attention to Victoria. "It'll be smart of you to stand clear of me. It's going to get bloody."

"It's already gotten bloody," Victoria complained to Vince. "How many more men will die? Five... ten? Twenty? How many more wooden boxes are you going to fill before your conscience is clear?"

"I ain't leaving until Miles Harter can live on his ranch in peace... when his boys can go to bed without fear their pa might be killed by the time they wake up," Vince answered without losing his patience with Victoria. "This ain't about me."

Victoria threw down a ripped rag and left the hot room she

was standing in. "She's a troubled woman," Sheriff Burke told Vince. "She came to this territory all torn up inside."

"Yeah... well, that's what war does to you." Vince excused himself, leaving Sheriff Burke alone with his wife.

Victoria was outside. Vince walked back to the jail and tended to his business. Winston and Gregory walked up to him like two slithery snakes.

"What is it?" Vince growled.

Judge Reed stepped out of the jail. He came to Vince's defense with a simple look. "Sheriff Dalby was ambushed. Had to shoot down some vile vermin. Durango should be grateful for such a man. Wouldn't you say, Mr. Drakes and Mr. Bells?"

Winston gritted his teeth. "Judge Reed, I respect your reputation and experience, but you are misled in regard to this man. He is a troublemaker who is out to serve his own agenda. His kind lost the war, and now he's out to kill any man who fought against him, while hiding behind a badge."

"A meeting has been called." Gregory spoke up in a cold voice. "By this time tomorrow, Mr. Dalby, you will be the one inside the jail."

"Not while I'm breathing," Judge Reed intervened. He walked to Vince and wiped some sweat off his leathery face. "This man is still the law, and I'm still a judge. McCook is still the territorial governor who stands for the law."

"Soon a state constitution will be drafted. Grant will issue a proclamation of statehood," Gregory remarked. "McCook will fail."

"Heard rumors Grant has his eye on a man named John Routt. Seems like you believe Mr. Drakes might take the job."

"Let's go." Gregory marched off with Winston.

Judge Reed narrowed his eyes. "You want to be careful of those two," he warned.

Before Vince could answer, he heard the sound of heavy

horses. Lattimere was riding into town with what hired guns he had left. "Looks like the snakes are all crawling out of the pit today."

Lattimere stopped his horse in front of the jail, studied the horses holding the bodies of his hired guns, and then rode on without saying a word. Vince knew what Lattimere's silence meant—he knew all too well. Blood was in the air. Vince's blood. But first Lattimere had business to take care of. John Dalton had to die.

Chapter Eight

Judge Reed had a change of heart about having supper with Vince. He suggested—in the strongest terms possible—that Vince get on his horse and take a ride out of town for the night. "This town is steaming hot. No telling what all the vermin walking about might be planning for tonight. It would be wise if you rode out of town."

"I'm not a coward—"

"Didn't say you were," Judge Reed cut Reed off in a sharp but careful tone. "You know how wars are fought. You're outnumbered right now. Just ride out of town, and let me be your eyes and ears."

Vince didn't like the idea of being run out of town. He was a fighter. Something in Judge Reed's eyes told Vince that, if didn't leave town, he might not live to see morning. A soldier knew when to fall back into the woods long enough to get his wits about him when the enemy became too much.

Lattimere had blood in his eyes. Winston and Gregory were working to rile up the town against Vince. Tempers were running hotter than a branding iron in the middle of July.

"Reckon it wouldn't hurt if I rode out and checked on my Miles Harter."

"You do that. I'll speak to the undertaker and get the bodies you brought into town taken care of." Judge Reed patted Vince on his shoulder and walked up the street.

A dozen hard men were standing outside the Burning Bullet Saloon, staring in Vince's direction. Gregory and Winston were inside the saloon.

Vince checked the street. He spotted Lattimere's horse in front of Andrew's law office. Well, technically, the law office belonged to his dead brother. Vince guessed Andrew would either pack up and move out or take over for his brother. "Yeah... you best play fair, boy. Don't take in with Lattimere or you'll end up dead."

Vince checked his horse. The horse was tired. Riding out to Miles's ranch would require all the steam the horse had left. Vince hated to ride his horse so hard. He didn't have a choice.

"There he goes," a man with black teeth hollered into the Burning Bullet Saloon after spitting a wad of tobacco out of his filthy mouth. "Riding out of town."

Winston gulped down a glass of whiskey. "We need to kill him."

"Not with Judge Reed in town." Gregory sipped on a hot beer. "We have leverage in this town. We'll wait a bit and let the men get whiskeyed up, then send them out with a message the town won't be able to refuse."

"What message?" Winston asked.

Gregory leaned back in a creaky wooden chair and grinned. "Obey or suffer the consequence," he answered. "By this time tomorrow, Vince Dalby will be enemy number one in Durango."

Winston looked about. He came across dirty faces that

seemed to have no soul. Fellas, who would sell their souls for a drink of whiskey. Gregory had managed to round up a mess of sharp horns who were either out of work, too thirty for whiskey to work, or too hungry for blood to care.

All the sour weeds present had walked in through the back door, unseen and unheard. "Are you sure you can control these men?"

"Lattimere isn't the only man in this territory who can run a stampede when needed," Gregory answered. "People in Animas are paying Lattimere protection money. Maybe it's time the people in Durango get shook up a little as well... and learn who the real boss is."

Crandal McCain, a dirty trail snake sitting close to Winston and Gregory, listened and then slipped out into the bright sun without causing any attention to himself. He found Lattimere buying a room at the hotel. "We need to talk."

Lattimere looked into the eyes of Crandal. The lobby of the hotel was bare. He nodded at a skittish clerk who stood behind the front counter. "Take a walk."

"Yes, Mr. Lattimere." The clerk nervously wandered off to perform some chore or another.

Lattimere placed a hand down onto his gun. "What have you got?"

"Bells and Drakes got a lot of hired hands to hit the town hard tonight. Some of those hired hands are gonna gun you down." While Crandal spoke, he fixed himself a quirley. "Bells and Drakes want you dead. They want Dalton left alive."

"Dalton slipped out of town. Andrew Tames seems to know where Dalton is, but he won't talk. He's too angry over his brother. I'm giving him time to cool down."

"Don't give that boy too much time because, come tomorrow, you might not be standing in your boots," Crandal warned.

"Bells has some brains in his head. He knows how to run a wild herd."

Lattimere gritted his teeth. "I have to thin out the herd some before I can kill Vince Dalby. If Dalby gets to Dalton, I'm cooked. I can't go off killing with Judge Reed in town. I've got a plan."

"Yeah?"

"I took Miles Harter's family," Lattimere told Crandal. "They're being held at my ranch. Miles will come looking for them. I let him live. Vince will be on his tail." Lattimere squeezed his gun as he talked. "They'll walk into an ambush. In the meantime, I'll stay in town and deal with Bells and his lame bull."

"Word is they intend to kill you and pin the murder on Dalby." Crandal talked in a calm, shadowy voice. He wasn't much for killing with a gun. He liked to kill with his knife. He wanted Vince's scalp—but Vince's scalp would be one saddlebag prize Crandal would have to pass up. "Let me deal with Bells and Drakes. You get out of town and deal with Vince."

"What's in it for you, Crandal? What's your angle?"

"I want in on the big prize. Lots of gold up in the San Juan Mountains. Railroad has claims on some mighty rich land. Cut me in for a share, and I'll get rid of Bells and Drakes." Crandal stamped out his quirley. "Most of your best guns are dead. Looks like you need a fella who knows how to step past his own grave."

Lattimere sneered. "What makes you think I'll cut you in?"

"Better to have me on your side." Crandal spoke in a challenging voice.

Lattimere studied Crandal's eyes for a long minute. "I'll pay you what you earn."

"Good enough."

"Get rid of Bells and his lame bull. No questions asked. Make sure no one sees the bodies."

"Good enough." Crandal scanned the hotel lobby with careful eyes and then walked outside.

As soon as Crandal was gone, two men walked out of a dusty dining room. "Let Crandall kill Bells and Drakes and then get rid of him," Lattimere ordered. "When night arrives, I'm riding out of town. Have my horse waiting outside of town. I don't want anyone seeing me ride out."

"You sure Dalby will fall for your trap?" one of the men asked.

"One way or the other, Dalby died tonight." Lattimere squeezed his gun again. "He'll follow Miles right into his death. If he doesn't, then we'll go hunting for him." Lattimere checked the time. It was almost supper. Time to eat. He had a long night ahead of him.

* * *

Victoria waited for Lattimere to walk to the dining room before sneaking out of the hotel. She had heard every word Lattimere had spoken. She hurried and found Judge Reed talking to Sheriff Burke. "Vince is going to walk into a trap," Victoria fretted.

Sheriff Burke was still too weak to even sit up. Doc Cunningham was away, seeing a rancher.

Only Judge Reed was in the room with Victoria and Sheriff Burke. He rubbed his chin for a long minute and then reached for a brown handkerchief in order to wipe sweat off the back of his neck. "Vince Dalby ain't a stupid man," he told Victoria. "He won't walk into a trap."

"What are you thinking?" Sheriff Burke asked Judge Reed, fearing the words that would be spoken.

"The way I see it," Judge Reed answered without hiding his mind, "is that it's best if we let the vermin die. I have a witness right here that has stated that Lattimere has ordered the death of Bells and Drakes. So be it. As for Lattimere... Vince is riding out to Miles's ranch right now. He'll find the truth and then deal with Lattimere accordingly. If we're blessed, by this time tomorrow, this territory will be free of a few bad snakes."

"Drakes and Bells have their hands in a lot of pockets," Sheriff Burke warned.

"Maybe so, but when they turn up deader than a rotted trail snake, the other vermin will back off. Death has a good way of making a fella realize he ain't gonna live forever. The grave has a mighty strange way of sobering a fella up." Judge Reed stopped wiping the back of his neck. The room he was standing in was hotter than blazes. "We'll just see how death plays out in this town tonight. Come morning, I have a feeling that whoever rides into town will be the one to claim the prize."

"If Lattimere—" Victoria began to agonize.

Judge Reed held up his hand. "In this part of the land," he cautioned, "there's only so much the law can do. If Vince meets his end, then so be it. I'll go after Lattimere myself based on what you said. If Bells and Drakes escape death, then... well... it'll be what it'll be. That's just the way it is."

Victoria threw her eyes at Sheriff Burke.

Sheriff Burke knew Judge Reed said what needed to be said. "Victoria, go back to the hotel and stay there till morning," he ordered. "Don't ride after Vince."

"But—"

"If Lattimere or one of his hired guns catches you on the trail, you'll likely meet a bad end. Just stay at the hotel," Sheriff Burke demanded. "You know I'm telling the truth!"

Yes. Victoria knew Sheriff Burke was telling the truth. She was a beautiful woman. Beautiful women didn't ride alone on a dangerous trail. Lattimere's hired guns had already seen Victoria standing up for Vince. If they caught Victoria out on the trail... death would come painfully slow. "I'll be at the hotel."

"It'll be best if I go with you," Judge Reed told Victoria. "We'll have supper. Best if I keep an eye on you."

"Good idea," Sheriff Burke agreed. "Doc Cunningham will be back shortly. My wife will be along shortly, too."

Judge Reed checked to make sure Sheriff Burke had plenty of drinking water sitting in a drinking pot while Victoria checked his stomach bandage. Once those chores were complete, the room emptied out. Sheriff Burke closed his eyes and began to pray.

* * *

Vince didn't hear Sheriff Burke praying. His ears were on the long trail standing before him. The ride to Miles's ranch was tedious and tiring. The trail was ripe for another ambush. Would Lattimere strike?

Vince rode slowly and carefully, careful not to push his horse too hard while keeping his rifle at the ready. His neck ached and throbbed. So be it. He was used to being hurt. What mattered was taking down his enemies. No matter the cost.

By the time Vince reached Miles's ranch, the sun was slipping down. The sight of pale stars was already beginning to appear overhead. Vince didn't need the last of the daylight to lead him to Miles's ranch.

The smell of smoke wrapped around him like heavy prison chains. Vince kicked his horse into a full run. When he came up on Miles's ranch, he saw the house burning. Miles was sitting on a rock about a hundred yards from the ranch house, loading his rifle.

"Lattimere took my family." Miles spoke in a deadly voice as soon as Vince jumped down off his horse. "I'm going after him."

Vince stared at the burning ranch house. Dead horses were crumpled on the ground close to the ranch house. He looked at Miles. Dried blood was caked all over Miles's face. "Miles—"

"I was left alive to tell you to leave or my family will be shot." Miles continued to load his rifle. "They shot the horses. I buried this rifle with some bullets a while back. Figured I might be needing it if my rifle was ever lost or taken."

Vince stared at the burning ranch house. Miles's entire life was going up in flames.

"I was told Lattimere would let my family go if you left town. Ain't so. He's gonna kill me off... kill my sons... and take Lauretta for himself. Ain't gonna let that happen."

"Lattimere will know you're—"

"Yeah, he'll know... He wants me to come for my family 'cause he wants me dead." Miles finished loading his rifle. "I was told to ride into town and tell you. Now that you're here... you with me?"

"You know I am..."

The sound of an approaching horse caused Vince to turn his head. It didn't take a second to spot Andrew Tames riding up. Peter Hauls was with him.

Miles didn't stand up. He locked his eyes on the burning ranch house. How many memories were going up in flames? Miles felt like he had been thrown into a deep grave.

"Miles..." Peter tried to speak but failed for words as his eyes watched flames lick up toward the stars.

"Mr. Harter, this has to end!" Andrew demanded. "I was on my way back to Durango when Mr. Hauls and I smelled the smoke."

"What's your business in Durango, Pete?" Miles asked Peter.

Peter was wearing what Miles called fightin' clothes. The man was holding a rifle and carrying the look of a fella who knew it was either time to fight or die. "Saw what they did to Jim, Miles... and now this," Peter answered in an angry voice. "Just this morning, some of Lattimere's hired guns came to collect money from me. I didn't have any to give. I was taken out back and horse-whipped, and then my store was kicked apart."

"Mr. Dalby," Andrew spoke up, "I need to speak frankly with you."

"Yeah... sure." Vince nodded.

"I'm not who I seem to be. Neither was my brother. We are both lawyers, yes, but we work for a firm back east that is against the railroad. Our job was to gather hard evidence against John Dalton and Stephen McQuire. You see, another railroad was supposed to have been created, Mr. Dalby. Certain illegal transactions are feared to have been carried out that prevented the railroad in question from taking form—"

"Get to the point," Vince ordered. Andrew was obviously an educated fellow. Vince wanted a simple version instead of a winded storm.

"Art Lattimere was given money by the railroad in question to prevent the current railroad from acquiring valuable land. Mr. Lattimere betrayed the trust given to him. In fact, he had killed, in cold blood, the very men who my brother and I were working for. With my brother's death, I now realize I have a choice: leave or die. I have talked Mr. Hauls into speaking with Judge Reed before I leave, in the hopes of putting a thorn in Mr. Lattimere's side."

"John Dalton ordered your brother to be killed—"

"Mr. Dalby, John Dalton is under Mr. Lattimere's control," Andrew insisted. "I played my part very well. I believed I had my foes deceived, as did my brother. We were wrong." Andrew bowed his head. "Terribly wrong."

Vince dared to look at Andrew. The man was sitting on a worn down quarter horse, broken and bitter. Lattimere was winning the war. "What does Lattimere want? Full control of the railroad?"

"Yes," Andrew answered. "The railroad and the land. He wants to own the mines and run tons of cattle. The cattle will be cover for hiring outlaws who will make sure he faces no opposition. And ultimately," Andrew finished with a bitter tone, "he wants to become governor."

"Yeah..."

Andrew watched the ranch house burn. "I came across John Dalton on the trail, Mr. Dalby. He's riding back east as fast as he can. Art Lattimere won't be seeing the likes of him again. I talked Mr. Dalton into meeting me in Boston. Maybe we can hurt Mr. Lattimere from there? I'm not sure. What I am sure of is that Mr. Lattimere intended to kill Mr. Dalton. Stephen McQuire can be controlled. Mr. Dalton is what you might call a wild bullet. He took a liking to a whore who Mr. Lattimere was controlling. Mr. Lattimere killed the whore and buried her body. Mr. Dalton's watch, dress shirt, and a few letters from his wife are buried with the whore."

"Lattimere will try to bring Dalton down," Miles said in a low growl.

"Yes, but Mr. Dalton intends to claim Mr. Lattimere was attempting to frame him... bully him into breaking the law, if you will. His running away to Boston will seem like a desperate escape from a ruthless killer," Andrew explained.

Vince didn't have time to worry about a no-good like John Dalton. "Take Hauls into town. Talk to Judge Reed," he ordered Andrew. "Have Judge Reed send a wire to the sheriff at Boulder Corner. Dalton will probably stop there when he gets tired."

"Miles... Lauretta and the boys?" Peter asked before riding off.

"Lattimere took them."

A heavy groan left Peter's mouth. "Miles..."

"Pete, don't," Miles growled. "You wanted to bow down to Lattimere... You wanted Vince to ride on. Now look." Miles stood up. He spit blood out of his mouth. "Was the beating worth it, Pete? Was the beating I took worth it? Are we yellow bellies?"

"Miles!"

"Ride on, Pete!" Miles pointed toward Durango. "Don't look back."

"No... wait... don't ride on," Vince ordered.

"What do you mean?" Miles asked.

Vince locked eyes with Peter. "Andrew, ride on... Don't look back. Go."

"But I need Mr. Hauls—"

"Mr. Hauls will be in Durango come morning. Now ride on and go find Judge Reed," Vince said in a tone that caused Andrew to give his horse a kick. Vince waited until Andrew rode off and then turned his mind to Peter. "Ready to fight?" he asked.

"What do you mean?" Peter asked as night began to settle harder and harder. Shadowy flames were now dancing on the man's back.

"You owe Lattimere money?" Vince asked.

"Protection money. I have till morning to pay up."

"What are you thinking?" Miles asked Vince.

"Lattimere will be expecting us tonight," Vince explained as the smell of burning wood suffocated his nose. "We won't play that hand. We'll wait till morning comes. When Lattimere sees we haven't showed up, he won't know what to suspect. Maybe he'll think you rode off to get some lawman from another town?

Lattimere was in town when I rode off. He'll know I've come out here."

"So?" Miles asked in a voice that grew impatient.

"Lattimere took your family but rode into town... or maybe that's the way he wants it to seem? Saw him go into the hotel..." Vince kept his eyes on the burning ranch house as he talked. "We won't play into his hand."

"Why can't we just tell somebody Lattimere took Lauretta and the boys?" Peter began to insist.

"Because the snakes who beat me didn't tell me Lattimere was behind the beating," Miles snapped at Peter. "You'd have to be a fool not to know, and Lattimere knows I ain't no fool! He's been wanting Lauretta for a long time... He knows I'll be gunning for him!"

"But if we don't show up tonight, then come morning he might just be sitting worried in his saddle," Vince told Miles. Best to make him sweat some. In the meantime..." Vince turned to face Peter. "You best be prepared to get your jaws to working because, come morning, the folks around here are either gonna stand up and fight or live yellow."

Peter stiffened in his saddle. "I reckon the time has come then, hasn't it?"

Vince nodded. "When you get through running your jaw tonight, you're gonna ride out to Lattimere's ranch and spread the word that you I stopped in Animas with Miles. Say I had Miles's body over a horse. Say I stopped at your store and woke you to get some rope to tie Miles's body. Say I shot him by mistake and I'm taking his body away but I'll be back come morning. Make it seem real important like... in order to get on Lattimere's good side. Say I threatened you if you rode off to run your mouth."

"You want to lead Lattimere into a trap," Miles told Vince.

Vince nodded. "Tell Lattimere you saw John Dalton meet

me outside and agree to meet me back in Animas come morning. Say John Dalton was real scared and wanted me to protect him. Say Andrew Tames will be with John Dalton."

"And then what?" Peter asked.

"Then the folks around this part will be hiding in town with their rifles ready to fight," Vince answered. "Blood for blood. That's the way it is. Blood for blood."

Chapter Nine

Lattimere sat down in front of a beautiful woman. Lauretta Harter didn't seem like the kind of woman who would marry a man like Miles. She was striking. The type of woman who could complement Lattimere in his quest to have absolute power. "It doesn't have to be this way," Lattimere said in a surprisingly sober voice. Getting all whiskeyed up wasn't the answer. Vince was sure to show up sooner or later. Lattimere wanted to be stone sober when he killed Vince.

"You made a mistake by not killing Miles. He will come for you," Lauretta snapped at Lattimere. She was sitting on a fancy couch that felt rough under her body. Logan and Jonas were tied up in an outside barn.

"Miles is a pathetic—"

"My husband is going to kill you." By now, Lauretta had the living room she was trapped in memorized. She knew how many steps it would take her to run to the front door, the windows, the door leading to the kitchen. Escape wasn't impossible. Lattimere wouldn't shoot Lauretta in the back. The hired guns standing guard outside would. Lauretta didn't doubt that.

Besides, she had her sons to think about. Surely Miles would be coming soon. Miles was most likely working out some sort of plan with Vince. There was no way in Lauretta's mind a man like Vince would walk away. That's what Lattimere was counting on.

Lattimere continued to stare at Lauretta. "Look at you... wearing a poor woman's dress. I could provide you with all the fancy dresses you want."

"You burned down my home. You beat my husband to an inch of his life. You have my two sons tied up outside. Given the chance, I would kill you without thinking twice."

Lattimere gritted his teeth. Lauretta meant her words. "You'll come to your senses."

"When? After you kill my sons?"

Lattimere's entire face changed from angry to trapped. Yeah, he was going to kill Logan and Jonas. What could he say? He couldn't leave Miles's boys alive. They would grow up and come gunning for him. "I'll be outside."

"The hounds of hell are coming for your soul," Lauretta warned Lattimere. "They are going to drag your worthless soul into the hottest of fires. Wait and see."

Lattimere grabbed Lauretta's face with a vicious hand before he could catch himself. "You shut your mouth!" he hollered.

Lauretta only grinned. "You'd better go dig your grave, Lattimere. My husband is coming for you."

Lattimere squeezed Lauretta's face and then stormed outside into a dry, hot night. "Anything?" he asked.

"Nothing," a man named Willy answered. "I've checked around. No one has come up the road or tried to sneak in through the fields."

"It's getting late. Vince will show up." Lattimere surveyed the night. His eyes went to a large barn that had been turned into a jail cell for Logan and Jonas. "Those boys giving you any trouble?"

"Nah. They're settled down."

"Keep an eye on them." Lattimere looked around again and then began to go back inside. As he did, the sound of an approaching horse caught his ear. He went for his gun and waited. A minute later, a man rode up. Two armed guns were behind him. "Peter Hauls... what are you doing here?" Lattimere demanded.

"Vince Dalby came to my store... woke me up... Well, I wasn't sleeping," Peter explained in a hurried voice that sounded anxious and a bit scared. "Mr. Lattimere, he needed rope."

"Rope?"

Peter had to make his act look as real as possible. "Vince Dalby done went and killed Miles, Mr. Lattimere. Said he shot Miles by mistake... thought Miles was one of your guys. He was waiting for John Dalton on the trail..." Peter raised a nervous hand. "I ain't a-lying, Mr. Lattimere. I saw Miles's body myself. Shot clean through the back."

Lattimere narrowed his eyes. "What else?" he barked.

"Just that John Dalton rode up... He and Vince Dalby agreed to meet back in town come morning. I heard John Dalton say Andrew Tames will be with him... something about how Tames is going to help him get to Boston. He is in Durango with Judge Reed... That's what John Dalton told Vince Dalby. Sorry if I don't got all the facts... I was tying Miles's body down on a horse I didn't recognize. Miles... dead... just can't believe it."

"And you're certain it was Miles?" Lattimere demanded.

"Mr. Lattimere, I could pick Miles out in a dust storm." Peter took off a brown hat and bowed his head. "Poor fella... What will Lauretta and the boys think?"

"Forget them!"

Peter startled. He put his hat back on. "Mr. Lattimere, I don't want no trouble. I done took a beating for not having your money... but I went around... Some friends gave me what they could. When your men come to see me come morning, I'll have some of the money... Vince Dalby will probably be in town. I just don't want you thinking I took sides with him."

"You just keep clear!" Lattimere pointed into the night. "Get riding. When you get back to your store, stay inside."

"Yes, Mr. Lattimere... and... about the money... I done got half, and—"

"Get to riding!" Lattimere roared.

Peter startled again. He gave his horse a kick and turned back the way he came, feeling grateful to be alive. Lattimere could have shot him off his saddle.

"Get the boys," Lattimere ordered Willy. "I want them in town before the sun rises. When Vince rides in, we'll wait. I want Vince, Dalton, and Tames all together." A vicious grin slipped across Lattimere's face. "Fate is being real good to me."

"What about the woman and her boys?" Willy asked.

"Not yet," Lattimere answered. "Just leave the boys tied up in the barn. I'll deal with them when the time is right."

* * *

Miles hunkered down behind a large tree with Vince at his side. "We can take them now."

"Too many. I've counted ten guns so far. If we spook Lattimere, he'll run. Just wait."

"You think Lattimere is going to ride off?"

"Yeah." Vince nodded. "When he rides off with his hired guns, we'll get your family." Vince squeezed Miles's shoulder. "You gotta trust me on this."

Miles kept his eyes on a large barn. He was sure that's

where his boys were being held. "You're standing at my side. Mighty grateful" was all he could say.

Vince checked his rifle and waited. No less than an hour later, he spotted Lattimere coming back outside.

"Kevin... Terry... you two stay here at the ranch and watch things. The rest of you ride out with me!"

"There they go," Miles whispered.

Vince watched Lattimere ride off with ten armed outlaws who, Vince knew, probably couldn't gun down a dead bull in a fair fight. Vince had killed off the best guns Lattimere had been able to hire. "I'll take out the two who stayed behind. When I do, get your wife and sons and ride south."

"I ain't leaving you—"

"I ain't arguing!" Vince grabbed Miles's shoulder with a hard hand. "I said—"

"And I said this is my fight!" Miles ripped away from Vince. "I'm gonna be the one to kill Lattimere, you hear me? Even if I wasn't gunning for Lattimere, I wouldn't ride off. Ain't right for a fella to turn yellow. You and me are friends now. I'll stand by you and die beside you if needed. Understand?"

Vince understood. He understood all too well. Miles was a good man. "Let's get your family."

"What's the plan?"

Vince nodded toward Lattimere's ranch house. "Watch 'em... They light up a quirley apiece and then stand around jabbing. One of them will eventually go for a whiskey bottle. We'll let them run loose on the rope before I go in for the kill."

Miles's patience was wearing thin, but he managed to wait and watch. And sure enough, the two guns did exactly as Vince said they would. "We got about an hour before morning. Time to move. When you see me kill those two, take for the barn. I'll take for the house."

"No... I'll kill them." Miles held up his rifle. "That's my family. You just cover me."

Vince wanted to object, but didn't. He knew. "Follow the tree line around. Get close to the house. Kill the first man. The second man will be taken off guard. He'll go for his gun or run. You'll have a couple of seconds to put him in your sights."

"I won't need no more than one."

Vince nodded. "I'll move close to the barn."

Miles got moving. His lame leg gave him trouble, but he didn't care. He moved as silently as an owl, slicing through the night air. His eyes were filled with rage. His heart filled with blood—finally understanding what drove Vince to kill without hesitation.

When Miles got as close to the ranch house as he could, he kneeled down on one knee. The night was dark. Two lanterns nailed to the outside of the front door of the ranch house gave light. Miles could see Lattimere's two guns standing in front of the ranch house, sharing a whiskey bottle.

"Time to die." Miles took aim at the first man and fired. A sizzling hot bullet tore through the man's heart. He hit the ground dead in his boots. The second man dropped the whiskey bottle he was holding.

Because of the whiskey, he wasn't able to think clearly. Instead of diving behind a nearby watering trough, he went for his gun. Miles pegged him in a second. The man dropped dead before he could blink. "Blood for blood."

Miles spotted Vince's shadow starting for the barn. He nodded and went for the house. He found Lauretta tied to a wooden chair.

"Miles!"

"Vince is going for the boys!" Miles hated that his lame leg was so much trouble. He nearly had to drag his leg into the living room.

"I can't get free. I've been fighting with these knots..."

"I'll cut you free." Miles put his rifle down and went for his hunting knife. He had Lauretta free in a minute. Without saying another word, he kissed his wife, picked up his rifle, and hurried back outside.

"Pa!"

"Logan... Jonas!" Miles kneeled next to two dead bodies as his boys ran into his arms.

"We knew you'd come, Pa! We just knew it!" Logan nearly cried as he hugged Miles. "Oh, Pa... forgive me... I don't mean to cry like a whipped horse."

"Son, it takes a real man to cry," Vince told Logan. He stood back and watched Miles pull his wife and sons into his arms as tightly as he could. "You can ride off."

"Ain't gonna." Miles shook his head. "Lauretta, take the boys and ride to Mary's. Stay there until I come for you."

"Pa?" Jonas asked in a worried voice. "You mean you ain't coming with us, Pa?"

"No, son. I'm going to go kill a snake." Miles bent low and rubbed his son's hair. "Your pa ain't yellow and never will be. See those two dead men...? I killed them, and I ain't ashamed that I did so, either. Your pa ain't no coward."

"You killed those two men, Pa?" Logan asked. Miles nodded. A proud smile touched Logan's eyes. "Ma, we best ride on. Pa has some more killin' to do."

"Yes, I know he does." Lauretta hugged her husband. "I'll be expecting you. We have a house to rebuild and a ranch to run."

Miles kissed Lauretta and then stepped back. "Take their horses and ride on. Jonas, ride with your ma. Logan, lead the way. Hug the trail and get into the trees if you hear any riders."

"And take this, son." Vince handed Logan one of his guns. "A man needs a gun."

Logan never felt prouder. "Okay, Ma... Jonas... Let's ride out."

Lauretta looked into Miles's eyes. "Come back to me."

"I plan to."

Vince and Miles watched Lauretta help Jonas up onto a saddled horse. Lauretta looked at Miles and then mounted up on the back of the saddle while Logan mounted another saddled horse. Together, they rode off into the night.

"We best get to that rock and see what man is willing to fight."

"I reckon so." Miles looked at Vince. "You're family now. Just saying." With those words, Miles walked off.

Vince nodded and followed. Death was still prowling about. By the time morning was in full bloom, Animas would be covered with dead bodies.

Vince wasn't sure if the men Peter had ridden out to talk to before taking for Lattimere's ranch would show up and fight or not. Each man was ordered to meet Vince at a high rock right before dawn. It wasn't too far from Animas, only a half-mile ride.

Deep down in his heart, Vince didn't expect a single man to show up. Would it matter? Could Vince and Miles kill Lattimere and his hired guns alone? An ambush, maybe. Vince and Miles were outgunned. So be it. Lattimere had to die.

When Vince rounded a curve attached to a back trail and came up on what Miles called a high rock, there wasn't a man or horse to be heard or seen. Vince walked his horse up to the rock. Miles followed with his head held low.

"Reckon we're going at it alone."

"Reckon so," Miles whispered, feeling mighty ashamed of his friends and neighbors. "We best ride. Got about half an hour of dark left."

"We'll take them the only way two fellas can. Gun to gun."

Miles looked at Vince. He could only see a shadow sitting on a saddle. "I might get pegged full of holes, but Lattimere will drown in his own blood before I do."

"Then let's ride."

Vince and Miles rode toward Animas. They stopped about a quarter mile from town and walked the rest of the way on foot. By then, the sun was peeking into the morning, giving enough light to make out the buildings.

Vince climbed up a tree and took a look. He spotted a few of Lattimere's hired guns hiding on wooden roofs. The rest of the hired guns were stationed inside of the buildings. He spotted Lattimere standing at a dusty window attached to Peter's store—waiting like a hungry wolf.

"What did you see?" Miles asked when Vince climbed down.

"Four men on the roofs. Lattimere is in Peter's store."

"What's your thinking on this?" Miles inquired as he checked his rifle. "Sun is going to be beating down on our neck real hard if we don't get to shooting."

"Horses are tied up behind Peter's store." Vince looked around. He and Miles were standing on a hill that let them have a good view of the town. Vince figured if he mustered himself back up a tree, he wouldn't have a problem picking off the hired guns stationed on the roofs. That was only four guns, though. Vince needed a distraction.

"Your mind is thinking. I can tell."

Vince nodded. "Come on."

Miles didn't ask any questions. He had learned to trust Vince.

Vince moved in a wide circle and managed to get around to the back of the town without being seen. He located a small herd of horses tied to a horse line. Through the woods, Vince could see the back side of Peter's store. "Gonna set the horses free. You get out of sight. When someone comes running for the horses, don't shoot."

"Reckon there's no time to argue." Miles quickly dragged himself behind a tree and got out of sight while Vince cut the horse line.

"Get!" Vince began slapping at the horses. The horses began fussing and bumping into each other, anxious to get free. The sound of the horses echoed into the town.

"Someone's getting at the horses," a man named Brushy hollered from one of the roofs.

Lattimere heard the horses fussing from inside Peter's store. Snakes got at horses as well as wild bears. Lattimere didn't want to jump to conclusions. "Go check the horses," he ordered Ron Taylor, a skinny fellow who was quicker on the draw than most of the men left under Lattimere's shadow.

Ron skedaddled out of a back door and ran into the trees.

Vince slid behind a tree and waited. When Ron showed up in the woods to check the horses, he launched out like a raging mountain lion. Ron turned just in time to see Vince lunge at him, holding a razor-sharp hunting knife.

Then Vince gigged the knife into Ron's chest, splicing through bone like a hot knife cutting through butter. Blood shot out from Ron's mouth. Miles had to turn his head.

Vince didn't have time to be timid. He killed Ron and then dragged the man's body behind a tree. Miles wasn't sure what Vince was thinking.

Vince took the dirty coat Ron had been wearing along with a filthy brown hat and made his way to Miles. "Put this on."

Miles quickly donned the coat and hat. "Keep your head low. The fella I just killed came out of Peter's store. Go for Lattimere. I'll handle the rest of the vermin."

"Just like that, huh?" Miles asked. "This war can end just

like that?" Miles looked into Vince's eyes. "I figured killing Lattimere would take a great deal of doing."

"Some battles last long and some don't. Just depends on the men fighting and how much guts they got. Most of the guns in town get tough only when they got other guns around." Vince stared into Miles's eyes for a long minute. "Lattimere took your family. Ain't right for a fella to do such a thing. Ain't right for me to kill him. You finish this. I'll be outside fighting for you."

"Reckon you will." Miles reached out and squeezed Vince's arm and then checked his rifle one last time. It was time for blood. "If I die, tell my family I didn't die yellow." With those words spoken, Miles started off toward town.

Vince didn't waste a second. He climbed up a tree and steadied himself against a limb. "Never thought I'd be up in a tree again." Vince quickly took aim at Brushy. He waited until Miles reached the back door of Peter's store and then fired. Brains splattered out of the back of Brushy's head. The single shot took the men on other roofs off guard.

Before the gun on the next roof could take a second breath, a bullet tore through his head. His body was flung off the roof he was standing on. Vince spotted the other two men running toward the back of the roofs they were standing on. He picked them off as Miles headed to Peter's store. The rest of the armed guns hiding in the stores came bursting out of the back doors with their guns blazing, just as Miles vanished into Peter's store.

Miles nearly bumped right into Lattimere, who shoved Miles aside as he jerked the back door open and began shooting.

All Lattimere saw was Ron step through the door with his head down. He didn't see the man's face. "You see anyone?" he yelled at Miles, thinking the man was Ron.

Miles watched Lattimere fire his gun at the woods and then stop to reload. "Yeah, I saw someone."

Lattimere froze when Miles's voice stabbed his ears.

Miles saw Lattimere's gun hand freeze. He slowly aimed his rifle at the man's back. "Turn around, Lattimere. Turn around and face me, or I'll peg you where you stand."

Lattimere slowly turned to face Miles. Miles had the drop on him. The rest of Lattimere's hired guns were busy firing at Vince. He heard one of his men yell, "He just gunned down Grant!"

Vince kept up his attack. Then, when he had to stop and reload, a bullet flew at him. The bullet ripped through the side of Vince's head like a raging bull goring an innocent child.

The force of the bullet caused Vince to lose his balance. His legs went out from under him. He tumbled out of the tree he was in and hit the ground harder than a rock.

"You got him!" one of Lattimere's guns yelled. "Young, you gunned him right out of that tree!"

A curious grin slipped across Lattimere's scared face. "You kill me and my men will gun you down."

Miles kept his eyes on Lattimere. Peter's body was lying on the floor close to the back door. The man's back was full of bullet holes. "I don't live yellow," he told Lattimere. Lattimere stopped grinning as the last of his guns ran off into the woods to finish Vince off.

"You don't got the guts, boy!" Lattimere spat at Miles. "You're nothing but trail waste!"

"Who killed Peter?"

"Who do you think?" Lattimere spat at Miles again. "I did! And I was going to kill your boys as soon as I finished with Vince Dalby! Then I was going to take your wife!"

Instead of losing his mind, Miles remained strangely calm. "My wife told me that the hounds of hell will be coming for your soul someday. That day has come."

"You don't got the guts!"

"I do!"

"What?" Lattimere turned his head just in time to see a woman with a bloody face aim a rifle at him and fire. The bullet torched the side of Lattimere's right cheek. The force of the bullet threw him backward. He tripped over Peter's body and hit the floor. Before he could go for his gun, Miles knocked him cold with his rifle. Part of Lattimere's skull cracked open, but he didn't die. Just sour blood—ugly, filthy, sour blood—began spilling out onto the dirty wooden floor.

"You're going to hang, Lattimere. Hang. A bullet is too merciful." Miles turned his attention to Peter's wife. The woman threw down her ride and ran to Peter. Lattimere had failed to kill her and left her tied up, thinking that was good enough.

Miles quickly focused back on Vince. Vince was hurt. Was he dead? Miles knew he couldn't just run off into the woods. He would be gunned down. He had Peter's wife to protect. Vince would stay and protect the woman.

Miles looked through the back door. He couldn't see too far into the woods from where he was standing. "Please, Lord," he prayed.

Vince shook his head just as three armed men circled around him with their guns, ready to kill. The world was spinning. He had hit his head really hard on the ground. He saw more than three men standing around him. Where was his rifle? Vince felt lost and disoriented.

"Well, look what we have here. Looks like we caught us a wounded rebel, boys."

Vince began searching the ground for his rifle with his right hand as the world continued to spin. For a minute, he thought he was back in the war. Then a hard boot kicked his hand.

"You gonna die real slow, boy—"

A bullet exploded. The snake who kicked Vince's hand was thrown forward. His body struck a tree and fell down. The last two guns standing around Vince spun around. A stampede of men were moving up into the woods with their rifles on fire. About ten men... all spread out in a line, firing like the dickens. Jim was leading the charge.

"Run!" one of the men tried to yell. A flood of bullets tore through his body and dropped him.

The last man tried to run. He didn't get far before his back was plugged full of holes.

Jim ran to Vince. "He's hurt!"

Miles heard Jim yell. "Oh praise God," he whispered. "Looks like we ain't yellow after all." Miles looked down at Peter's body as heavy, painful sobs came from the man's wife. "We won't ever be yellow again."

Vince didn't hear Miles. All he felt was a slew of hands pick him up and carry him into Peter's store—hands belonging to men who had finally decided it would be better to die than to live yellow and afraid of a man like Art Lattimere.

Chapter Ten

Lattimere roared as a jury pronounced him guilty. "You are to be hanged by the neck until you are dead!" Judge Reed yelled at Lattimere. "Get him back to the jail. The hanging will take place tomorrow at noon!"

A group of armed men grabbed Lattimere and dragged him out of a sweltering courtroom.

Lattimere yelled and hollered threats as he was dragged away. "You a dead man, Miles! Dead! This ain't over!"

Vince was standing at the back of the courtroom, leaning back against a wooden wall. When Lattimere reached Vince, he stopped. "I look forward to seeing you at the end of a rope," Vince told Lattimere.

"I'll see you in the fire, boy!" Lattimere spat at Vince.

"Just as long as I see you hang first." Vince nodded at the men holding Lattimere—men he had sworn in as faithful deputies. "Get him back to the jail and post guards."

When the courtroom cleared out, Miles walked up to Vince with his wife and two sons. "How's your head?"

"Hurts."

"I was mighty worried.

"I know." Vince looked at Lauretta and then at Logan and Jonas. Relief was now in their eyes. "What's the plan?" he asked.

"Rebuild. I don't intend to run," Miles answered.

Lauretta squeezed Miles's hand. "I begged Miles to take us away... My husband isn't a coward. If he left, he would never be able to live with himself. The same goes for all the men who stood up to Lattimere. If good people run away, then the bad win."

"Will you be leaving?" Miles asked Vince.

"When Sheriff Burke is able to wear his badge again, I reckon I'll move on." Vince touched the side of his head. Blood for blood—even his own blood—in order to bring peace to Miles and his family. "Why didn't you kill Lattimere?"

"A bullet was too good for him. A rope isn't," Miles answered.

Judge Reed walked up, wiping sweat off the back of his neck. "While you two were off fighting Lattimere, we had a real bloody night here in town." Judge Reed nodded at Lauretta and her sons. "Go take the boys to the hotel. Tell Mr. Smith to put your noon meal on my tab."

"That's mighty kind of you," Miles told Judge Reed. He smiled at Lauretta. "Go on. I'll be along shortly."

Lauretta knew her sons were hungry. She was hungry herself. "Judge Reed, it's very kind of you to pay for us to stay at the hotel until our ranch house is rebuilt. How can we ever repay you?'

"No need to." Judge Reed looked down at four innocent, staring eyes. "Your pa did real good, boys. Real good. You'll never have a reason not to be proud of him."

"Pa is the best," Logan exclaimed. "He can kill any outlaw there is."

"Well... maybe." Miles laughed and then scooted his family outside.

"You have a fine family," Judge Reed told Miles.

"I reckon I'm more blessed than I know."

Judge Reed's eyes turned serious. "Drakes and Bells were gunned down right on the street. The fella who gunned them down tried to get out of town. He didn't make it far before meeting his own end. Lattimere had a good plan in place."

"You could have stopped the killings," Vince told Judge Reed.

"Reckon I could have. I didn't." Judge Reed nodded toward Miles. "Vince, I'm a man who fights for the law... but there are times when the law of man is as flawed as a man's ability to understand his own face. Only God's law is perfect." Judge Reed let out a long breath that was filled with deep thoughts. "I've learned a thing or two in my years. What I've learned most is that sometimes you have to stand back and let the bullets fly how they will. If that pegs me as a guilty varmint, then so be it."

"Looks to me like you saved me and Miles a good deal of trouble. I wasn't sure how I was going to handle Drakes and Bells," Vince confessed.

"Vince, you tried to take on this war all by yourself. I have a bad feeling you did the same thing in the war you're still being held prisoner in." Judge Reed reached out and tapped Vince's chest. "You gotta learn you can't win a war all by yourself. No man can."

Vince didn't respond. He folded his arms over the black shirt he was wearing and waited. Judge Reed had more to stay.

"Vince, you're as deadly a man as I've ever seen," Judge Reed went on. "But someday you're going to slow down. You won't be quick at the draw. Some other man will be faster than you... meaner than you... stronger than you... and, yes, smarter than you. You need friends. Men who will stand by you... like Miles."

"You telling me to stay here?" Vince asked.

"Where else can you go? Down another trail?" Judge Reed inquired. "To another town where you'll kill again... and again... until you're killed yourself. And then what? I'll tell you what. Your body will be thrown into an empty grave that won't mean nothing. But you can change that." Judge Reed tapped Vince's chest again. "There's a mighty pretty woman in this town who is just as lost as you are. Maybe the two of you can find your way home together?"

Vince lowered his eyes. Judge Reed was talking about Victoria. "Yeah..."

Judge Reed turned and pointed at the hot courtroom he was standing in. He pointed to a line of chairs the jury had sat on. "Today, a group of men condemned a guilty man to his death. So what? Just because one bad man is going to hang doesn't mean they all will. You can't kill them all, Vince. There comes a time when a man has to stop running." Judge Reed left the courtroom without saying another word. He was hungry. Having a noontime meal with Miles's family seemed mighty nice.

"Judge Reed is right, you know," Miles told Vince. "I know it ain't my place to say so, but I was hoping you wouldn't ride off. You're family."

"You can't afford to work me at your ranch."

"Sheriff Burke may not put his badge back on."

Vince raised his eyes. "He said that?" he asked.

Miles nodded. "His wife wants him to take her back east. Doc Cunningham can't say for sure Sheriff Burke will ever be fully healed again."

"Burke is a good man."

"Yeah, he is, but he's got a wife, same as me." Miles grew

quiet for a couple of minutes as the heat buzzed in his ears. "Durango needs a good sheriff. Just saying," he told Vince, and then left the courtroom.

Vince stayed in the courtroom for a bit and then walked over to see Sheriff Burke. Victoria was tending to the man. "Lattimere is going to hang."

"I heard the news," Sheriff Burke replied in a relieved voice. "Got plenty of guards?"

"Plenty."

Victoria rinsed out a cold rag. "I'll be getting to the hotel for my meal."

"Uh..." Vince's deadly face softened in a way that shocked both Victoria and Sheriff Burke. "I was hoping maybe we could eat a meal together, ma'am. My belly has been rumbling something awful for the last few days."

A sigh left Victoria's mouth—so tender, like a morning rose petal falling to the ground. "Mr. Dalby, will you be leaving us soon?"

"I don't..." Vince began to answer and then stopped. He dropped his eyes down onto the badge hooked to the front of his shirt. "Ma'am, I'm having a hard time finding my way. But across the street at the hotel, there's a man with his family who are eating in peace and a piece of trail filth down at the jail waiting to meet his end. I reckon that's good enough for me."

"You did a good job, Vince... and you're going to continue to do a good job because I don't plan on being sheriff anymore," Sheriff Burke told Vince. "Wife wants to go back east. Reckon I best take her. You're now sheriff until you decide otherwise. Now that Drakes and Bells are dead, the town ain't gonna put up a fuss."

Before Vince could answer, a tall, skinny man hurried into the room Sheriff Burke was resting in. "Got a wire," he announced. "For Sheriff Dalby. Here."

Vince took the paper.

"What is it?" Victoria asked as darkness walked back into Vince's eyes.

"Michael Garland..."

"The gunslinger?" Sheriff Burke asked. Vince nodded. "Thought he ran down to Mexico after that posse got after him."

"He's been seen in the New Mexico Territory." Vince shoved the paper he was holding into a dusty pocket. He looked at Victoria. Victoria simply placed a wet washcloth on Sheriff Burke's head and left the room. The skinny man followed her.

"You riding out?" Sheriff Burke asked.

Vince wanted to ride out. He had dealings with Michael Garland that went way back.

Vince's silence told Sheriff Burke all he needed to know. "You gonna stay around long enough to see Lattimere hang?"

"Yeah." Vince no longer felt hungry. The sounds of dead men screaming broke into his mind. Each dead man was screaming for Vince to join them. "I'll be at the jail."

"What about Victoria?"

"I reckon our trails just weren't mean to cross."

Vince walked back to the jail. Lattimere was securely locked up. Vince took to his desk and waited as men began to build Lattimere's wooden hanging gallows outside. The sound of hammers striking nails echoed into Vince's mind as he thought about Michael Garland—as the screams of dead men tormented his mind.

When night fell, Lattimere began hollering from his jail cell.

Vince walked back to him under the guard of three men. "What is it?"

"I just wanted to see your face, Dalby... You look at me! I may hang, but you'll never win! You're no better than I am. Your hands are covered with blood!" Lattimere spat at Vince. "You already have a rope around your neck! When I hang, you'll watch my feet kick...

but it'll be your feet kicking, not mine!"

Vince stared into Lattimere's vicious eyes and then walked back to his desk. Victoria was waiting for him. She had a plate full of food in her hands. "Knew you'd be hungry. Need to eat before you ride out."

"Not riding out." Vince sat down behind his desk. "If Garland makes his way to Durango, I'll deal with him." Vince hated to tie himself down, but he knew that if he left, Victoria would suffer. Victoria was worth saving more than killing a man who Vince had grown up with and called a brother—a man Vince had fought in the war with.

"I see." Victoria sat the plate of food she was holding down onto the desk. She looked so beautiful in the green and white dress covering her frame—broken and still bitter... but desperate to find healing and peace.

"Absolution."

"What?" Victoria asked.

"I think I can find absolution here," Vince told Victoria as he picked up the fork sitting on his supper plate. A steak and a baked potato greeted Vince. Vince found a knife. "Mighty kind of you to bring me supper."

"Knew you would be hungry."

"I am," Vince confessed. "Mighty hungry in fact." Vince looked up into Victoria's eyes. "Thank you."

"Of course." Victoria didn't smile, but her voice turned soft. She left the jail and walked back to the hotel under a blanket of hot stars while Vince went to eating.

* * *

The following day at noon, Lattimere was dragged out to the hanging gallows. The entire town gathered to watch the man hang.

Peter's wife was standing as close to the gallows as possible. "Hang him!" she cried. "He killed my Peter in cold blood!"

Lauretta put her arms around the poor woman and waited.

Miles had the privilege of putting the noose around Lattimere's neck.

Lattimere spat at Miles. "I'll see you in the fire!"

"When the hounds of hell come for you, I'll be smiling," Miles told Lattimere as he tightened the noose. He then stepped back.

A preacher walked up to Lattimere. Lattimere spat at him. Judge Reed nodded at Vince. There was no sense in trying to show any mercy to Lattimere. The man's soul was condemned to the fire.

Vince checked the hanging rope. "Rope is secure."

"I'll see you in the fire!" Lattimere yelled. "All of you!"

Vince nodded at Miles. Miles pulled a wooden lever. The wooden door Lattimere was standing on burst open like the sound of a dead man waking from his grave. Lattimere's large body dropped like a heavy rock. Miles's son watched as Lattimere's legs jerked and kicked... jerked and kicked... until he was dead.

"Let this be a lesson," Judge Reed said in a loud voice. "Good men are no longer going to tolerate law breakers. If It comes down to blood for blood, then so be it!" Judge Reed pointed at the Burning Bullet Saloon. "I can't close that door to hell, but I swear that any man who dares leave that place to break the law will end up at the end of a rope!"

The dirty snakes standing in the crowd looked around at each other. Lattimere was dead. Almost all of his hired guns were dead. Durango was no longer being controlled by outlaws.

It was time to ride on. The Burning Bullet Saloon could burn as far as they cared.

After the hanging, Miles found Vince in the jail. "Riding out to the ranch."

"Figured you would."

"You riding out, too?"

"Just for a bit," Vince answered as he checked his guns. "Got a second wire. Michael Garland killed two deputies. Seems he's heading this way. Don't want him getting too close to Durango. Leaving you in charge until I get back."

"I can ride with you..."

"Not this time." The tone in Vince's voice told Miles to stand down. "This is between me and Garland. We go way back."

"I'll be back in town tomorrow."

Vince nodded. He walked outside to his horse and began checking his saddle and rifle. "I'll be back," Vince told Miles as he mounted up. "If I don't come back, you're sheriff."

Miles put a hand over his eyes and looked up at Vince. Vince still had blood in his eyes. Maybe someday, Miles thought, Vince might be able to wipe the blood out of his eyes— but not anytime soon. "Be prayin' for you."

"Appreciate that." Vince looked up the street toward the hotel. Victoria was watching him. He nodded and rode off into the heat... prepared for more blood.

Miles walked up the street to the hotel. He joined Victoria.

"Will he come back?" Victoria dared to ask.

"Yeah... he'll come back," Miles answered as Vince vanished like a dark shadow slipping into the heart of the sun. "He'll come back, but the war in his heart still won't be over." Miles shook his head and walked into the hotel to fetch his family.

Victoria looked down the street and waited. "Maybe some-day... we can end the war together."

Vince didn't hear Victoria. His mind was on Michael Garland. "Blood for blood, Garland... That's how we do it this time... blood for blood. This time you won't escape."

Far away, sitting up in a spill of dry rocks smoking a quirley, Michael Garland waited for Vince.

Blood for blood. A new war. A new battle. Only one man would walk out alive.

The End

More westerns are in the works.
I would appreciate a positive review on Amazon.

Made in the USA
Columbia, SC
10 June 2025

59223142R00076